SPECIAL MESSAGE TO READERS

THE ULVERSCROFT FOUNDATION
(registered UK charity number 264873)
was established in 1972 to provide funds for
research, diagnosis and treatment of eye diseases.
Examples of major projects funded by
the Ulverscroft Foundation are:-

- The Children's Eye Unit at Moorfields Eye Hospital, London
- The Ulverscroft Children's Eye Unit at Great Ormond Street Hospital for Sick Children
- Funding research into eye diseases and treatment at the Department of Ophthalmology, University of Leicester
- The Ulverscroft Vision Research Group, Institute of Child Health
- Twin operating theatres at the Western Ophthalmic Hospital, London
- The Chair of Ophthalmology at the Royal Australian College of Ophthalmologists

You can help further the work of the Foundation
by making a donation or leaving a legacy.
Every contribution is gratefully received. If you
would like to help support the Foundation or
require further information, please contact:

THE ULVERSCROFT FOUNDATION
The Green, Bradgate Road, Anstey
Leicester LE7 7FU, England
Tel: (0116) 236 4325

website: www.foundation.ulverscroft.com

THE CARING HEART

Caro has always looked after her niece Rose, who is like a sister to her. With Rose threatened by an unpayable rent increase, Caro heads off to the Hovercombe Manor estate to support her and sort things out. On her way, she meets Liam Tait, the attractive new owner of the Manor, and starts to fall for him. But the scheming of the unpleasant estate manager Jared, and the arrival of Liam's gorgeous friend Elissa, both spell trouble for Caro . . .

SHEILA SPENCER-SMITH

THE CARING HEART

Complete and Unabridged

LINFORD
Leicester

First published in Great Britain in 2018

First Linford Edition
published 2018

A catalogue record for this book is available
from the British Library.

ISBN 978–1–4448–3583–0

Published by
F. A. Thorpe (Publishing)
Anstey, Leicestershire

Set by Words & Graphics Ltd.
Anstey, Leicestershire
Printed and bound in Great Britain by
T. J. International Ltd., Padstow, Cornwall

This book is printed on acid-free paper

1

The dentist's receptionist opened the outside door and stood to one side.

'It's a beautiful day out there,' she said in her cultured voice.

Caro tried to reply but ended up making some sort of grimace. The receptionist, smiling, seemed not to notice. A kind girl, Caro thought, obviously used to patients with frozen mouths anxious only to get home before the effect of the injections wore off.

'Goodbye, Miss Anderson. We'll see you in September.'

'Goodbye.' There, that was better. She had managed that. Heartened, Caro stood straighter now and held the brass handrail only lightly as she went down the steps.

The day was indeed lovely. Sunshine reflected from the windows of the shop opposite and the flowers outside the florist's next door were glowing in the light that slanted through the awning above. On impulse, she lifted a dripping bunch of pinks from their bucket and carried it into the shop to make her purchase. The assistant here was smiling too as she took them from Caro and placed them on a sheet of navy tissue paper that emphasised the pure white of the blooms. Two friendly people, happy in their work, Caro thought, and tried to smile back.

'A present for someone?' the assistant asked, interested.

'Well yes, my niece.'

'Your niece?' A slight inflection of surprise in her voice. 'Lucky girl.'

Caro's eye danced. She was used to this reaction. There weren't many years between herself and Rose — six in fact. They were more like sisters.

'Yes, but . . . Sorry. The dentist — '

'Oh dear. Poor you. It sounds as if you need these more than she does.'

More than Rose? The misplaced

sympathy was almost too much, and Caro took a moment to reply. She'd had toothache, that was all; and once the immediate soreness of the extraction was over, all would be well. But Rose —

'Oh no, really not,' she said with difficulty.

Out in the bright street again, she stood on the edge of the pavement waiting for a gap in the traffic. Even the fumes couldn't quite swamp the heady scent of the flowers, and Caro held them to her nose, feeling the warmth of the early spring sunshine on her face and the hope in her heart that in some small way these flowers would raise a smile of something like pleasure in Rose.

She felt her jaw as she reached her car, anxious now to get home and take some painkillers before discomfort set in. She had promised herself an early start, but then this tooth problem had flared up. All a bit of a shock, really.

'It'll need to come out,' the dentist

had said as she sat imprisoned in his chair. 'I can do it now if you like.'

Caro had agreed hurriedly before she changed her mind. Getting it over and done with was an advantage if she was going to be any help to Rose. So now she would be only a little late in setting out. With luck, she would manage to make up the time on her drive to Rose's remote Devon valley. Midweek in early March. Yes, she could do it.

* * *

Fluffy wasn't really a problem. Sandy next door had agreed to see he didn't starve while she was away, and had already purchased some tins of Catalux, his favourite food of the moment.

'I'll pretend he's mine. You know how I love him.' Sandy grinned. 'And going into your place to feed him.'

'You'll pretend that's yours as well?' Caro smiled too. This was Sandy's usual reaction, and had become a running joke between them. They both knew there was a grain of truth in it because the two cottages could so easily be converted into one.

'I'll look after him like my own.'

Lap of luxury were the words that sprang to Caro's mind as she unlocked the back door and Fluffy came purring out to greet her.

'Cupboard love,' she told him, edging him away with her foot in order to make a dash for her packet of paracetamol in the kitchen cupboard. 'All right, I'll feed you before I go.'

She bent to stroke his long, soft fur, so thick that beneath it he seemed no more than a taut collection of bone, half the size of the finished animal. She had promised the dentist she would rest before setting out on her journey, and so she would. Outside, she perched on the low wall and moved along a little to make room for Fluffy, who was purring even more lustily now, his breath smelling of fish.

Ten minutes was surely long enough to sit about doing nothing. Rose's voice had been full of tears when Caro phoned her yesterday evening.

'Rose?' Caro's breath was tight in her throat as she considered the possibilities for her vulnerable two-year-old nephew. 'Jonah? Has something happened to Jonah?'

Rose took a deep breath.

'No, no . . . it's not Jonah.' Rose's voice still had a wobble, although it was obvious she was trying to control it. 'I've had this letter, you see.'

'A letter?'

'From the new agent, Jared Butler.'

'And?'

'He wants to double my rent.'

'But he can't do that!'

'He says . . . ' Rose broke off; and then, after taking a gulp of air, 'He says he's got to make the estate more profitable. But I can't afford it, Caro.'

Her voice had a helplessness to it that wrung at Caro's heart. This new agent must surely have been told that Rose's young husband had been the chauffeur to the estate, as well as performing other duties, and had been highly thought of by old Mrs Tait before the fatal accident ten months ago that had been no fault of his own. So what was this man thinking of, when Rose should surely have been given special treatment in the circumstances? In fact, it had been promised to her. It was clear that Rose needed a champion.

With her hand over the mouthpiece, Caro sighed, considering.

'Are you still there?' A sob from Rose.

'Don't worry, Rose,' Caro said as calmly as she could. 'I'll come down and give you some support. I need to sort out a few things here tomorrow morning, and then I'll be on my way.'

'Oh, would you?' There was a lightness to Rose's voice now.

Caro smiled. 'Of course. Haven't I always been there for you? Of course I'll come.'

So now her bag was already packed and waiting. Thank goodness she had delivered another selection of her botanical paintings to the gallery in Dorchester, and hadn't yet started on her new project. There was nothing really pressing that needed attention for a day or two.

2

At Exeter, Caro took the A30, glad to get past this stretch of it as she always was because of her elder brother and his wife's fatal accident here years ago. It had been fortunate that their two-year-old daughter wasn't with them. Even now she shivered in horror of how different the lives of several people would have been if baby Rose had died with her parents.

The muddy river smell was what she remembered most about the day Rose came to live with them. No settling down on the bank at Dad's side with his fishing tackle to hand that dreadful morning. That was extraordinary in itself. Her feet had slid on the muddy path because it had rained the night before, a torrential downpour that had caused the accident, and now Rose didn't have a mummy and daddy of her own . . . and that had made her feel guilty, because she had two parents and Rose hadn't any. She'd known Dad's mind wasn't on her as she slithered along beside him. He was thinking of the uproar at home as Mum, shocked and compassionate, prepared to collect the orphaned toddler while Dad was taking ten-year-old Caro for her favourite walk. Oh, she had thought in desperation, why couldn't everything go back to the way it was!

Rose's hair had been pure auburn gold as she stood in the doorway of the conservatory at home with the light behind her and her teddy bear in one arm. He had one eye missing and his jacket had one sleeve dangling too. Caro saw an expression so vulnerable in the little girl who was to be her sister from now on that it tore at her heart.

Where was Blue Ted now? Caro wondered as she put her foot down on the accelerator. Consigned to the bin, she supposed, and not kept for little Jonah. Last Christmas she had bought him a golden teddy bear of his own, but he didn't carry it round with him as Rose had done with Blue Ted.

She was past the accident spot now, and well on her way. Too soon for another painkiller? She felt a trickle of something in her mouth. Blood? She felt dizzy at the thought. She must do something quickly — but the tissue in the back pocket of her jeans was inaccessible. The car swerved a little as she tried to get to it. Oops! But what was that up ahead? A mini service station she had often noticed but never used appeared just at the right moment. With great care she drove into the forecourt and chose the nearest empty space.

At once she was out of the car with a tissue held to her mouth while the ground swayed around her.

'Can I be of assistance?'

The voice was friendly, registering concern. She looked up and saw a tall man whose short dark hair seemed to spring out from his head above his ears.

11

There was a warmth about him that, with his laid-back smile, seemed to inspire confidence.

'My tooth.' The relief to confide in someone made her voice tremble.

'You've knocked it?'

She shook her head.

'It's not there any more,' she mumbled. 'It's been taken out.'

Dismayed, she felt herself stumble, and at once his arm was round her.

'Here, sit down.'

She sank down, half-in and half-out of her car with its door hanging open. She felt the offending tissue whipped out of her hand and replaced with something cool and soft that she presumed was his handkerchief.

'Press it on the gap,' he said. 'And hold it down hard.'

'Thank you.'

'And don't move. It'll stop in a moment.'

Caro did as he said, breathing deeply.

'Better now?'

'I . . . I think so.'

He looked at her quizzically.

'Wait there.'

He was back in a moment with a box of tissues. Through a mist of uncertainty she watched him extract one.

'We'll wait a moment to make sure the bleeding has stopped, and then apply this instead. More convenient for driving. Have you far to go?'

'I turn off the main road in about twenty minutes,' she mumbled.

He seemed to make out her words, indistinct though they were. He folded a tissue into a small wad and exchanged it for his handkerchief.

'How about a hot drink before you set off? They do a good coffee here.' Gone was the sympathy in his voice now, but his eyes looked kind. He would be in a hurry to be off — a business appointment, perhaps — and she had held him up.

She shook her head. The dentist had warned her off hot liquids for the moment, and that was one rule she was going to obey.

'I can't. It's not good for it. Sorry.'

'Right, then. I'm heading in the same direction as you. I'll drive behind you until you turn off.'

'Oh!' For a moment she felt dizzy again.

'Something wrong?'

'I've forgotten the pinks,' she said, dismayed.

'Pinks? Flowers, you mean?'

'For my sister, my niece.'

His mouth quirked at the corners.

'You're not too sure?'

'White pinks with a lovely scent.'

As if it mattered what colour they were. He must think her stupid — which indeed she was for leaving them on the kitchen table, having meant to soak them in water while she fed Fluffy. Speaking clearly was difficult, too, with a wodge of tissue pressed to where her offending tooth had been.

He obviously realised this, and she was grateful for the sympathetic pat on her shoulders. He would make a good friend, she thought; capable of kind and appropriate action when needed.

'Not to worry. Wait here again if you will.'

She moved the tissue a little, and then daringly removed it. She took a quick look and saw to her relief that there was only a smidgeon of blood on it, nothing at all to be scared of. Hastily, she took another tissue from the box. The bin was nearby, so disposing of the used one was easy.

He was back now, looking pleased with himself as he held out a bunch of lilies in bud.

'I couldn't get pinks. Will these do instead? The girl said they're white ones, so I thought you wouldn't mind.'

She smiled, and hoped it wasn't merely a grimace

'That's so kind of you.'

'You sister-niece will like them, d'you think?' He sounded as if it was a matter of great importance.

'Who wouldn't? They're beautiful.'

He smiled too.

'Then let's go.'

His car was a white soft-top, and the roof was down. As they set off, Caro saw that he kept a convenient distance behind her. She signalled well in advance of her turning and he gave a cheerful farewell wave. Only then did she realise that she didn't know his name, or how to contact him to thank him for his help. She hadn't been thinking straight — and all because of a faint hint of blood that anyone with any sense would have ignored.

3

A fitful sun was shining as Caro drove down the narrow single-tracked lane that led to Hover Cottage. Before getting out of her vehicle she hastily removed the tissue from her mouth.

Rose was in the garden and came running out to greet her. 'Caro!'

'You're alone? Where's Jonah?

'Still asleep.'

Relieved, Caro gave her a quick hug before turning to reach into the car. 'Here, these are for you.'

'Oh!' Rose's face lit up. She sniffed at the lilies. 'They're beautiful.'

Caro smiled too. Impressive, perhaps, she thought as she carried her bag up the stone path; but in their present closed-bud state, hardly beautiful.

Rose paused as they reached the door, smiling a little shyly.

'I've got a visitor I'd like you to meet, Caro.'

'A visitor?' This was a surprise.

'He's not staying long.'

Intrigued, Caro followed Rose into the dimness of the cottage. She put her bag down in the passage and they went into the living room.

'This is Arnold,' Rose said. 'You remember him, Caro?' Her face was slightly flushed and her eyes bright.

He rose from his chair, a stocky man in a brown jacket. As they shook hands he gave Caro an odd look.

'Tom's cousin,' he said, 'or second cousin, if you prefer. Something like that, anyway. Just passing through on my way to Falmouth.'

His handshake was firm, but his smile was brief and didn't quite reach his eyes. Caro remembered him now from the funeral, where his dark clothes had made him seem far older and rather detached. She had been a little in awe of him.

'Rose has got herself a pleasant

18

enough place here.' Again, the quick smile that wasn't quite a smile. 'She tells me it was once two cottages knocked into one. Interesting that half the roof is thatched, and the other half tiled. It's only the second time I've seen it.' He let out a sigh. 'Yes, I could be happy here, I told her.'

Rose said nothing, but Caro could see that she was a little disconcerted. Who was this man anyway, turning up out of the blue? She wasn't sure she liked the idea.

'Arnold's been living in London,' Rose said by way of explanation when he had taken his leave. 'I'd never met him before the funeral. He didn't come to our wedding.'

'Perhaps he wasn't invited?'

'Tom was short of relatives. I think he would have been.'

The sad look was back in Rose's eyes now, and she drooped a little. Seeing it, Caro tried to be positive, even though she felt wary of his motives. Maybe she was being too protective, but Rose was

19

vulnerable still, and it was up to her to look out for her.

'Well, it's a good thing he's turned up now, isn't it?' she said. 'You can do with all the support you can get.'

Rose brightened.

'He was so interested in the cottage when I showed him round. That was before I put Jonah down.'

Caro glanced at the cuckoo clock on the wall between the two deep-set windows.

'So, he's been here some time?'

'Well, yes, I suppose he must have been.'

Rose was still holding the lilies. There was a distant cry.

'Jonah,' she said, instantly alert. 'You get the flowers in water while I see to him,' she added, thrusting them at Caro.

Caro knew where Rose kept the vases, and selected a tall green one that would set the white flowers off to perfection when they were fully in bloom. She filled it with water and then pulled off the cellophane wrapping.

But what was this?

Inside was a card, pushed down among the stems so it couldn't be missed. She fished it out and read the words inscribed on it in gold copperplate print.

Liam Tait,
Consultant in Garden Design,
Hovercombe Manor, Hovercombe,
Okehampton, Devon. EX20 6YX.

On the other side, hastily written in pencil, were the words, *Safe journey and may we meet again soon! Liam.*

Caro stared at the message until sounds from the passage alerted her to Rose's return with young Jonah. She stuffed the card in the pocket of her jeans, quickly arranged the lilies, and followed Rose and her two-year-old son into the living-room where Rose sat down with Jonah on her lap. He leaned back against her, still bleary with sleep.

Caro looked for somewhere to put

the vase. The pot-bellied stove stood on a granite slab in the wide recess. Since it was unlit, the space beside it would be perfect since there was just enough room.

'There!'

'They're lovely,' Rose said.

Caro seated herself close to her so she could stroke Jonah's soft cheek. She smiled as he edged away from her.

'I must let him get used to me again once he's woken up properly.'

'He knows his Aunty Caro, don't you, my pet?' Rose crooned, rocking him backwards and forwards. 'Look at the pretty flowers, Jonah.'

'Flowers?' Jonah said, wide-eyed now.

'There were meant to be pinks,' Caro explained. 'That's what I bought you in the florist's.'

'So, what happened?'

Caro smiled, amused that Rose didn't seem at all surprised. From her childhood she had been used to Caro's flights of fancy, and obviously thought that this was one of them.

'Would you be astonished to learn that a man I met on the way down bought them for you?'

'For me?'

'I told him I'd got some pinks for you but left them behind. So, he got these instead.'

'But what happened to the pinks?'

'You don't mean to say that you wanted the pinks as well as the lilies?' Caro laughed, trying to imagine Rose being pushy and grasping but not succeeding.

But Rose wasn't listening. There were the sounds of footsteps outside now, and then a peremptory knock on the door.

'I'll go, shall I?' Caro leapt up.

But Rose had got up too and was handing Jonah to her. The little boy clung on tightly, at the same time straining away from her to get to his mother. But Rose was out of the room talking to somebody on the porch. Her voice was hardly more than a mumble, but the other person, a man, was making his position clear in a way that sounded unfriendly.

Caro sighed. Should she do something? But no. There was Jonah to consider and she would be better attending to him instead of letting him witness a confrontation that sounded unpleasant.

The lid of his toy-box, over in the corner, was half-open. 'So, what are we going to play with, Jonah?' she said, putting him down on the floor and kneeling by his side.

He hesitated for a moment, then pulled out a battered white rabbit that had seen better days, and reached for a book underneath. He looked triumphant as he waved it at her.

'Book!'

'Let me see?'

But he wasn't having any of that.

'Hey,' she said laughing, as he held it tight against him. 'Aren't you going to show me the pictures?'

Apparently not.

'Cat,' he said, grinning at her, his

eyes shining with delight. 'Jonah's cat.'

Immediately Caro thought of Fluffy and those pinks she'd left on the kitchen table. She'd give Sandy a ring in a minute and explain.

The outside door slammed and Rose returned to the room, her face pale. She shivered.

'That was Jared Butler, on his way out somewhere for the rest of the day.'

'The agent? What did he want, Rose? It sounded as if he was threatening you.'

Rose gave herself a little shake.

'Not really. He always sounds like that.' She bit her lip. 'He was just checking, that's all. He needs to know what I'm going to do.'

'So, he's harassing you?' Rose hadn't been given notice to quit, but had merely been notified of the intended rent rise. Why was this man coming on to her like this? It wasn't right.

'I don't know . . . ' Rose started to say. Her eyes followed her son, who was now walking about the room, holding his book as if he suspected that someone was going to snatch it from him.

The living room was charming, with its low ceiling, wide inglenook fireplace, and the warmth from the radiator making it seem extra cosy. At one end, the floor was a little higher. Tom had made wooden steps from one level to the other, and erected a wooden balustrade to separate the two parts. The higher one contained the dining table and chairs. Since Caro was here last, Rose had had a stairgate fixed to keep a prowling toddler out. No wonder she was loath to leave, Caro thought, even if she hadn't felt the need to remain for Tom's mother's sake. Poor Enid, confused and helpless, couldn't be moved now from the security of her care home, and Rose liked to visit her nearly every day.

Jonah sat down on the top step and opened his book.

'He looks a real little professor,' Caro said.

Rose looked pleased. 'D'you think so?'

'He'll go far, your son.'

'D'you think Tom would have been proud of him?' Rose sounded so wistful it was pitiful.

'Of course he would. And of you, too, Rose.'

There was a minute's tense silence and then Jonah let out a screech.

'He's hungry,' Rose said. 'I'd better do something about lunch, hadn't I? There's some soup and a new loaf from the shop. Will that do?'

'It sounds perfect.'

Jonah thought so too as he sat in his high chair at the table with Caro and Rose on either side of him.

Caro glanced out of the small window now at the trees and the green, rounding hills, all so peaceful and remote. So how did Liam Tait, Consultant in Garden Design, fit in? She slipped her hand in her pocket and fingered the card, as she had done many times since she'd put it there yesterday.

Afterwards, Rose produced fruit, and a delicious apple cake that had come from the resident cook of the manor house in one of her bursts of generosity.

'Cindy's fond of Jonah,' Rose said as if that explained everything. 'Not everyone likes her, but she's kind to us. You've seen the house, haven't you, Caro, when we took you there on an Open Day before Jonah was born? The old lady lived there then.'

Caro remembered Hovercombe Manor very well. The June day had been warm, and they had sat on the terrace in deep basket chairs, eating lemon drizzle cake and drinking copious cups of tea. Sunlight had reflected on the mullioned windows of the stone building behind them, and Tom had leaned back in his chair looking supremely content.

The old lady had never married, and there had never been talk of any relatives as far as she knew. Rose seemed to know nothing of the new owner although her friend, the house-keeper and cook at the Manor, must surely have.

The Open Day visit must have been four years ago at least, and a lot had occurred in the meantime. Caro's aunt had died, leaving the bulk of her estate to her. With it she had purchased her home in Bridport, welcoming the chance it gave her to concentrate full-time on her art and yet still be within reasonable distance of Rose. She was able to travel to London fairly easily too to see her agent and exhibit her botanical paintings in the galleries that were beginning to seek out her work. Without it, her struggle would have been hard indeed.

'It all happened quickly at the Manor in the end,' Rose said. 'Since then, there have been builders and decorators in.'

'So, there'll be changes?'

Rose's face clouded.

'When she became ill, Mrs Tait appointed Jared Butler in a hurry, so that there would some sort of continuity.'

'The wrong sort,' Caro commented. 'Bully Butler sounds a horrible man. Is he married?'

Rose gave a little giggle. 'There you go, matchmaking again.'

Caro smiled too. This sounded like the old Rose.

As they cleared away, Rose told her about the day the letter came about the proposed rent rise, and how devastated she'd felt.

'But you said nothing to me at the time.'

Rose dried her hands and reached up to the wall cupboard to put the pepper and salt away.

'I'll show you the letter,' she said.

In the sitting room, Jonah was busy with three more books. He laid them out on the floor in front of him and gave every impression that he was studying each one deeply. His fair curly head was bent, and the back of his neck looked so tender and vulnerable Caro had to struggle not to lean forward and kiss it.

The letter was blunt and to the point. No waster of words, this Jared Butler.

'I am instructed to inform you that economic reasons make it neces- sary to raise the rent of Hover Cottage, to take effect from Lady Day,' Caro read out loud. *'Please call at the estate office for final details. I trust this will cause no inconvenience.'*

'No inconvenience?' Rose said bit- terly.

'So, you did?'

Rose nodded.

'I took Jonah in the pushchair.' She paused for a moment, remembering. 'Jared Butler wasn't there. But this was left for me.'

She handed Caro another piece of paper, thicker this time and with the address embossed in black lettering. On it was the proposed high increase in rent.

Caro whistled.

'But this is monstrous.'

'I know.'

'And what do the other tenants on the estate say about it?'

Rose looked unhappy.

'I don't know. I haven't asked them.'

Caro bit back an exasperated exclamation, remembering that the other properties, mainly farms, were some distance away from Hover Cottage. Apart from infrequent social occasions, Rose was unlikely to meet the tenants in her everyday life. There was the telephone, of course, but it seemed she hadn't thought of that.

The defeated look on Rose's face was back again and Caro knew she would have to tread carefully.

'Don't worry,' Caro said, her voice gentle. 'We'll get things sorted out between us while I'm here.'

First, though, she would unpack her few things and get settled in. The conversion of Hover Cottage into one larger home some years ago had been done so well that Caro found it hard, sometimes, to believe that once two families had lived here side by side. The indent in the wall in the main bedroom that had once been an outside door had been closed off and had shelves installed where Rose displayed family photos. One of them, larger than the others in its silver frame, had been taken on her wedding day. In it Tom stood proudly beside his new wife, the pretty and demure Rose ethereal in her lacy dress. It almost hurt Caro to look at it now, and she averted her eyes as she passed by on her way to the adjoining room that she always used when she came to stay.

As usual, she went straight to the window to gaze out at the enticing view of the wooded hillside, soon to be clothed in green when the trees took on their summer foliage. But this wouldn't do. There was unpacking to be done.

Back in the living room, she smiled to

see Rose sitting on the floor, apparently engrossed in her son's game of moving toy cars from one place to another. It seemed enough for Rose at the moment to have her there, and she must curb her impatience because Jared Butler wouldn't be at the Manor today. Her instinct was to get on with things immediately, while Rose's approach was to let things slide a little and see what happened. Caro sighed.

Rose looked up, startled.

'Something wrong?'

A great deal, Caro could have said, but she merely shrugged.

'It's so good of you to come,' Rose said. 'Nothing seems quite so bad with you here, Caro.'

She looked so earnest that Caro was touched. Rose shouldn't have to face this burden alone. She would do her best to convince Rose that Caro taking on Jared Butler on her behalf was the right thing to do.

4

'I thought I might go along and see Jared Butler this morning,' Caro said. They were seated at the breakfast table, and she leaned forward to cut a piece of toast into strips for Jonah, whose favourite food this was at the moment.

'Now?' Rose looked startled.

'The sooner the better, don't you think? I need to be home by tomorrow evening and there's not much time. Shall we go together?'

To Caro's relief Rose shook her head. Far better for her stay here to allow scope for some really hard talking. Jared Butler was an unknown quantity. For all she knew, he might be working under the orders of the new owner of the Manor, and not from Mrs Tait, who had been aware of the gratitude the estate owed poor Tom but had obviously failed to pass the information on.

'Could you take the cake tin back to Cindy for me?' Rose said. 'The housekeeper. She guards the door like a prison warder, but she'll let you in when she knows who you are.'

The set-up at the Manor seemed more dismaying by the minute between Bully Butler and this dragon Cindy. Add to that the new mystery owner, and it sounded as if she would be in for a good time.

'More, more, more?'

Jonah had finished his toast and was looking at his mother expectantly.

They both laughed, and the slightly tense moment was eased, so that by the time Caro set off she was feeling hopeful.

She decided to walk. For one thing, she loved the feeling that everything in nature was on the move, and wanted to feel part of it. She was pleased to see primroses in the grass along the hedge bottoms. For another, it gave her time to plan out what she was going to say to Jared Butler who couldn't seem to leave poor Rose alone. She must be tactful, of course, and friendly — even though she hadn't liked the sound of him yesterday. But, hey, she could manage that. She was used to asserting herself when dealing with the occasional gallery manager who assumed from her pleasant attitude and fair looks that she would be a walkover.

Her pace increased as she reached the start of the long drive that led down to the house. She was halfway along when she heard a car engine. A familiar white soft-top drew up alongside her and stopped.

'We meet again!'

His expression was one of pleasure rather than surprise. His dark hair framed his tanned face in a way she found attractive. She clutched the cake tin close to her as if she needed protection.

'Hello.'

'You were on your way to see me?' His eyes sparkled at her and she was aware that he knew exactly who she was.

'Caro Anderson,' she said. 'My sister lives in Hover Cottage. I'm staying with her.'

'Ah yes, the Lady of the Pinks.'

'Of the lilies,' she corrected.

'Of course, the lilies.'

She hesitated. He looked so relaxed sitting there with one hand on the steering wheel that it should have been easy to thank him for the help he had given her yesterday, but somehow the words wouldn't come. She cleared her throat.

He eyed the tin in her arms and raised one eyebrow.

'You have a present for me? No?'

'How would I know I'd meet you here?' she said crisply. 'Or even who you are? And why would I present you with an empty tin anyway?'

He acknowledged the sense of that with a quick bow.

'Liam Tait, new owner of Hovercombe Manor, with huge plans for the estate on my first visit as the legal owner. Will that do? Care to jump in, and we'll make a grand entrance together?'

'This is your first visit?' she asked suspiciously.

'With the keys in my hand and all perfectly legal since yesterday afternoon. I must admit, though, that I actually moved in with all my goods and chattels a little early. Mrs Tait's solicitor in Launceston will attest to it all being above-board; a kind and sympathetic man, with a lot of common sense. A new broom sweeping clean, that's me. You can come and hold my hand if you like. Why not?'

She hesitated.

'I held your hand yesterday,' he pointed out. 'Metaphorically speaking, of course.'

'I remember.' Suddenly she made up her mind. 'Repayment for your great kindness and generosity. It's a deal.'

'Then jump in.'

Smiling, she did as he said.

'So tell me, what brings you here?'

Her smile faded. It might well be that the proposed increase in rent was at his insistence and the agent merely obeying orders. She must tread carefully.

'Rose. My sister.'

'Or niece?'

'Both.' Let him make what he wanted of that. 'I'm hoping to see the agent, Jared Butler, on her behalf. She has a rent problem that needs sorting out.'

'I expect you know that the estate office is part of the house? Mrs Tait liked it that way apparently. No doubt he'll be there.'

He seemed perfectly at ease, but she was still suspicious. He pulled up at the bottom of the drive in the front of the house and got out. She'd forgotten how tall he was. That strange haircut seemed to indicate a shorter man, but she didn't quite know why.

The huge front door stood open and so his keys were not needed after all. He pocketed them without comment, ushered her inside, and indicated the door at the end of the wide passage on the left.

The ornate brass plate was polished to a high degree. The lettering on it said 'Estate Agent and Manager'; and then underneath, on a Post-it note, 'Please Knock'.

With a mischievous look at Caro, Liam knocked smartly and, without waiting for an answer, pushed the door open. There was no one inside.

'He had an appointment to meet me here.' He glanced at his watch and frowned.

There was nothing Caro could say to that, and so she remained silent. She noticed that on the wall above the desk was a line of framed certificates. Jared Butler advertising his credentials? If so, it seemed he was well-qualified, but not exactly punctual.

'I'll check with the housekeeper.'

They returned to the hall, and Liam pressed the bell on the table that stood against one wall with a pile of papers on it. He flipped through them while they waited.

Another door burst open and a girl in a blue apron appeared. Her brown hair was tied back from her round face and held in position with a brown band.

'Yes?'

'Cindy.' Liam said, swinging round. 'Do you know anything about this? Jared is not in his room.'

Her eyes flicked to Caro and then back again.

'This is my guest, Caro Anderson.'

'Are you wanting me to prepare another bedroom?' Her voice was like ice.

'That won't be necessary.'

'I see.'

No, she didn't, Caro thought, biting back a smile. Liam's face was serious, but from the little she knew of him, that could mean nothing. A secret joke? Could be.

'Jared Butler?' he said. 'D'you know his whereabouts, Cindy? We need to see him.'

Cindy shrugged.

'Best phone him.'

Liam's smile was brief.

'Thank you, Cindy. I'll do just that. Coffee, I think? And some of those shortbread biscuits of yours. Outside on the terrace as it's a good day. Is that all right with you, Caro?

She nodded.

'Thank you.'

'It's the least I can do since you've been disappointed in your quest,' he said when they had settled themselves in the basket chairs Caro remembered from her earlier visit.

On the way out to the terrace, Liam had shown her the stained-glass window in the small room near the front door, and while she admired the vivid colouring and design he spoke on his mobile. The sharpness in his voice boded ill for the absent Jared. Liam was not pleased with what he was hearing, that was clear, and she felt a shiver of uneasiness as she listened to him.

Now, sitting here in the sunshine, he smiled pleasantly at her. Before them on the low table was the tray Cindy had dumped there. In her mind Caro could still hear the rattling of the crockery reverberating in the air. Cindy had made her feelings only too clear, and by the speed she had answered Liam's request for refreshments, she had indicated that she wished Caro to be gone as soon as she had swallowed the hot coffee Liam was now pouring into the dainty decorated mugs.

He handed her mug to her and she exclaimed in pleasure at the design of a tulip in delicate pinks and reds on one side of it.

'You like it'

'Exquisite,' she murmured.

'They belonged to my late relative,' he said. 'I hardly knew of her, I'm afraid. She was my grandmother's much younger adopted sister, and for some reason we never met. And then on her death all this was all left to me. It was a total shock.'

The house was in a hollow, and the surrounding grassland and wooded hills seemed to hover protectively around it.

Nearer at hand, someone had cut the lawn, and a show of daffodils shone golden in the sunshine. She imagined more beds full of multi-coloured tulips in a week or two.

'It all looks so beautiful,' she said.

'But with little scope for improvement. I'm disappointed about that.' She remembered the card pushed down among the lilies.

'So, you're a landscape gardener?'

'Specialising in garden design on a grand scale when the opportunity offers. It means travelling a lot at the moment, often abroad. And you, Caro? What is it you do, apart from visiting your mystery relation?'

'Rose is no mystery,' she said with spirit. 'She's lived in Hover Cottage since she and Tom got married. I'm a botanical artist. Freelance. At least . . . ' She felt her eyes cloud. 'I've been offered a contract, an important one. A London Gallery, The Clover — '

'I've heard of it.'

'You have?'

'The prestigious one in Gower Yard? I went here once with a friend to attend the opening ceremony. A couple of years ago, I think. You must be good.'

She didn't want to talk about it or this contract, the best she'd been offered since leaving art college, and the sort of thing she had been working towards for the last few years. Much research on her part must be done during the summer months, and the work produced before the deadline — fortunately not until the end of the year, as she had other work on hand too. All this would be totally time-consuming. But for the moment there were other issues to think about. If only she could get to see this Jared Butler . . . But now it seemed that it was going to be difficult, if not impossible, before she had to return home. She frowned.

'So the agent won't be here today?' she said, her voice rough with disappointment. 'I have to leave here tomorrow evening at the latest.'

'Would you like me to put your case to him?'

'You would do that?'

'I'll have to know the details, though.'

He listened carefully as Caro told him about Tom's work as Mrs Tait's chauffeur, and of how much she had valued his kindness to her. He had been her right-hand man in so many ways.

'Tom died about six months ago,' she said. 'The accident wasn't his fault.'

'And Rose was left a widow?'

'With a young child. Rose hates the thought of leaving here, but with the huge rent increase she might have to.'

He looked startled. 'Rent increase?'

'That's what the letter from the agent says.'

Liam's eyes narrowed. 'Was any reason given for that?'

'To make the estate pay, apparently.'

He drummed his fingers on the table top, then opened the lid of the coffee pot to peer inside. 'More coffee?'

She shook her head. 'No thanks.'

'Another biscuit?'

Again she declined. They were melt-in-the-mouth delicious, but she felt another would choke her.

She hesitated for a moment and then spoke quickly. She felt she was telling tales out of school, but there was Rose's welfare to consider.

'You see, Mrs Tait told Rose that her rent should stay the same for as long as she wished to stay.'

'*Should* or *would*?'

Caro sat quite still, staring at him. Rose had been hazy about the actual wording, but obviously believed that the promise should hold good. And now this man, who had inherited the estate and the responsibilities that went with it, was seated opposite her and must be convinced about the truth of it all.

She took a deep breath, ready to put all she could in pleading Rose's case. Liam leaned forward as she spoke, his head held a little to one side as he listened. There was silence for a moment when Caro finished. Her words seemed to echo in her head and she could hardly breathe.

'I understand,' he said at last.

She looked at him then, weak with relief.

He stirred a little in his seat, and she was reminded that he was a busy man. It was time for her to go. She pushed her chair back and stood up.

He got to his feet too and smiled at her.

'Leave it with me. I shall do what I can. May I have your mobile number?'

She gave it to him, and as she turned away she saw the tin placed on one of the empty chairs.

'I need to give this to your housekeeper.'

His mobile phone rang.

'Ah,' he said, checking the screen. 'This will be important. I'll take this now, if you don't mind. The kitchen is opposite the library. She'll be in there, I expect.'

5

Caro found Cindy rolling out pastry on the wooden table in the centre of the large room. There was a patch of flour on one cheek that gave her a rakish look. She glared at Caro as she noticed the tin held out to her.

'What's that?'

'Rose asked me to return it.'

'Leave it over there then.' With a floury hand, Cindy indicated the dresser on the far wall.

This wasn't easy with the stacks of jars and kitchen implements on every crowded surface, but Caro wasn't going to argue. She turned to go.

'So Rose is in on this affair, is she? I thought better of her than that.' Cindy's voice was so accusing that Caro halted. What was it with these people connected with the estate? Not Liam, of course. A sudden vision of his teasing eyes made her bite back the first comment that sprang to her lips.

'You've got it wrong,' she said. 'It's nothing like you imagine. Nothing at all.'

Cindy's irate expression didn't change, and Caro didn't wait for more.

Out in the fresh air, the world seemed a different place. Liam had vanished on some business of his own, and the sooner she was out of here, the better. The primroses in the grassy banks looked as lovely as before, but she couldn't feel their beauty because of the housekeeper's sharp words. It was clear that she regarded her as an enemy, and that hurt.

The money she had inherited from Auntie Maggie had all gone, or she would have had plenty available to help Rose financially. The day four years ago when her aunt had told her of her will was another that stuck firmly in her memory. Because the older woman had been standing with her back to the French doors in her apartment, Caro couldn't quite make out her expression, but she sensed that her usual stern countenance had softened a little.

'I've always cared for you, Caro,' she had said. 'My special niece, my god-daughter, and now I want to make amends.'

'Amends?'

'Oh, nothing I've done, you may be sure of that. No, it's the way you've always had to look out for young Rose, my great-niece. And now you'll soon be on your own again, with that young man of yours going off to the States without you — '

For a moment Caro had been silenced. Rob had tried and failed to understand that she needed to look out for Rose. Their relationship was never going to work. They had both agreed on that.

'It's my chance to even things up,' Aunt Maggie said. 'And that's why it's all coming to you, Caro, apart from the handsome cheque Rose will have when she marries Tom in a couple of weeks.'

She laughed as Caro gaped at her.

'It won't be for many a year yet, I hope; but when I'm gone it's all yours, Caro. All of it. I know how much you want to be a successful botanical artist, my dear, and my money is to help you on your way.'

'But we're sisters, Rose and me. We have been since we adopted her — '

Auntie Maggie raised her thick eyebrows.

'Adopted? I think not.'

'As good as.' The intention had been clear, anyway. Rose was her sister. Her niece as well, of course, her late brother George's daughter. They were sisters in all but fact, and had always shared everything.

Sadly, Aunt Maggie hadn't lived much longer; but long enough for Rose and Tom to receive the wedding present that had been promised to them, and which had made it possible for them to have the honeymoon of their dreams. Of Rose's dreams, anyway, and no one wanted to deprive her of that, least of all Tom. Caro smiled now as she remembered Rose's shining eyes at the thought of tropical beaches on the other side of the world for a glorious three weeks of sun and sea. Was it better, Caro wondered, to have that one wonderful time with the man you loved; or to put that money by for a rainy day, a time when that man was no longer there to share it with you? But no one could see into the future, and who could blame Rose? Her home was secure on the estate as she and Tom settled down to a life together, and when Aunt Maggie's will was read, she was delighted for Caro, and urged her in the purchasing of the property that made such a difference to her way of life.

* * *

Liam's mobile phone call was not so important after all. His client's secretary was speaking for him, postponing the meeting arranged for tomorrow until the Wednesday of next week. This meant that he had extra time to perfect the plans without feeling the need to rush them. He had hoped the call was a prospective new client making enquiries on what he could deliver as a landscape gardener, but that might come at any time, and meanwhile he had some sorting-out to do.

His study was on the first floor, a large sunny room he had earmarked for the purpose on his first visit a few weeks ago. There was ample space for the oversized table in the middle of the room. Here he laid out the plans he was working on for the latest project. There was room, too, for his desk and storage chests. He took the stairs two at time and arrived at the door as the phone on his desk began to ring.

He leaned across to pick up the receiver and carried it across to the window.

'Jared?'

The voice on the other end was matter-of-fact, and Liam listened for a moment, his face impassive. The man had gone almost too far this time, taking time off without notification, and then having the gall to pretend he was on estate business, presuming his new boss hadn't yet had time to realise the true position. *Play it cool, man*, Liam admonished himself. Time enough in the next few days to reinforce job descriptions on a more legal footing.

'I need you back here later today,' he said, his voice crisp. 'There's an estate matter that needs your attention and must be dealt with immediately. Shall we say nine sharp this evening in the office? I shall expect you then.'

He replaced the receiver and sat down at his desk. Then he picked up his pen and tapped it on his teeth, deep in thought. Once or twice he had had occasion to doubt the man's dealings concerning estate matters, but his predecessor had trusted him, and for her sake he was willing to overlook the few times this had happened in the hope that Jared Butler would settle down and eventually prove his worth. A new broom sweeping clean, he had told his visitor as they drove the short distance to the house. She had looked amused, obviously thinking he was joking. True, of course, and he certainly didn't want to be doing that. The matter she had raised, though, definitely required attention from him. He liked her direct and trusting gaze as she confided in him, and the way she had sat quite still for a few moments when he had promised he would look into it.

6

Rose seemed almost relieved that nothing definite had come of Caro's visit to Hovercombe Manor. Caro found her in the garden, pegging out Jonah's clothes on the rotating washing-line. A red jersey with a teddy bear appliquéd to the front looked colourful beside the denim trousers and light blue shirt on either side. Rose's cheeks were a little flushed, and she was humming softly to herself until she noticed Caro watching her.

'I've just put him down,' she said in explanation before Caro had a chance to ask where Jonah was.

'Time for a rest for you, then?'

'Did you see Jared?'

'I saw Liam Tait.'

'Oh?'

Rose's eyes widened and she looked as if she didn't want to hear any more.

It had been clear earlier that she was uneasy about the agent being contacted, and now she felt this was worse.

'It's all right, Rose. Don't worry.'

'What did he say?'

'We had coffee out on the terrace, but his housekeeper didn't like me being there one little bit. It was a wonder she didn't slip something nasty into the coffee or poison those luscious biscuits.'

Rose giggled. 'That's not Cindy's way. She says everything to your face, outspoken, that's her.'

'And actions speak louder than words,' Caro said with feeling. 'Banging things about, thumping the tray down and glaring at me.'

'How did Mr Tait take it?'

'Laid-back, ignoring her. He seems as great a guy as I thought yesterday. I'm ready for another coffee if you haven't had one yet. Out here? Oh, but what about Jonah?'

Rose picked up the empty clothes basket. 'He'll sleep for an hour at least and the baby alarm's on. I'll hear him.'

'Then why don't you get the garden chairs out while I make the coffee?' Caro took the basket from her. 'Trust me, Rose.'

'As if I didn't,' Rose said.

They sat near the hedge that bordered the lane, a convenient place for hearing the latch on the gate that meant a visitor. Caro knew it was far too soon to be notified that Rose's rent problem was over, but she couldn't quite relax, and suspected that Rose felt the same.

Rose leaned over and picked a piece of long grass. Thoughtfully, she nibbled the white piece at the base of the stem.

'I do so love being here.'

'It's beautiful.' Caro leaned back in her chair and closed her eyes. The sunshine felt balmy on her face and birdsong was the only sound. The faint smell of coffee mingled with the moist scent of crushed grass. She could work here, she thought, undisturbed by the disruptions of modern life. Fluffy would love it, too with an exciting hunting ground close by.

'You were going to tell me — ' Rose began.

'Oh, yes.' Caro opened her eyes and sat up. She reached for her coffee, took a sip, and put the mug down again. 'Our man is still away, it appears, so I couldn't see him. But Liam phoned him, none too pleased. Bully Butler might be in for a shock when he gets back.'

Rose stared at her, wide-eyed. 'Oh.'

'And the good news is that Liam understood your position when I told him. He wanted to know all the details, and I believe he'll do something about it.'

'That's good, isn't it?' Rose sounded doubtful.

'Of course. It's going to be all right, Rose, you see. They say if you want anything done you should go straight to the top. Lucky for me that Bully Butler hadn't got back yet, and I was in the right place at the right time.'

Rose smiled too, happy now that Caro's visit to the Manor on her behalf had gone well. Looking at her, relaxing in the sunshine, Caro felt a surge of love tinged with guilt.

'If I hadn't got the money from Aunt Maggie all tied up, I could have helped out financially,' she said.

Rose shook her head. 'That's yours. I couldn't take it.'

'Not even to save your home in a place you love?'

'I could get a job.'

They both knew this was most unlikely. In a rural area like this, jobs were hard to come by, and there was young Jonah to consider. Cindy was Rose's friend, but she was already working so that was no good. She hadn't sounded very friendly towards Rose an hour or two ago either. Get Jonah into her clutches and goodness knew what might happen. Caro shuddered.

The hard part now was waiting to hear the outcome of her visit to the

Manor. Once Jonah was awake, they must do something interesting to give themselves something else to think about.

'Let's go out,' Caro said, 'as soon as Jonah surfaces. What do you say, Rose? Anywhere special you'd like to go?'

Rose picked another piece of long grass, looked at it, and then threw it down again.

'In the car?' She sounded dismayed.

There was a good village shop in Hovercombe about a mile away, and Rose did her shopping there. Afterwards, she and Jonah would call in on the Care Home on one of her frequent visits to Tom's mother. She walked there and back in all weathers because she wouldn't accept a lift from anyone since Tom's accident.

'We needn't go far,' Caro said gently. 'Tavistock? I'd love to go there again and Jonah would like the park.'

'The swings — '

'And lots more.'

Rose hesitated, obviously struggling.

Caro looked away, concentrating on a couple of wood pigeons on one of the higher branches of the young oak on the far side of the garden.

'I haven't been to Tavistock for ages,' Rose said quietly.

'Then that's settled. Or shall we wait and see what Jonah has to say about it?'

Rose's answering giggle was cheering, and for the rest of the time they both relaxed a little. The March sunlight was pleasant in this sheltered spot, and Caro's natural optimism reasserted itself. Liam would override his agent's decision about the rent rise. He was the owner, after all. There was nothing to worry about.

'We'll get some lunch in Tavistock,' she said. 'Make a day of it. Does that sound good to you?'

'Oh, yes. And there'll be time when we get back to call on Enid. Jonah loves seeing his Nana.'

'And you do too?'

Rose smiled and nodded.

'We talk about Tom, you see.'

Something must have woken her early next morning. It was dark still, and no sound disturbed the quiet air, yet Caro's heart was pounding. She switched on her torch. Six-fifteen! A mug of good hot tea — oh, yes please! Soon Jonah would be stirring in his little room on the other side of the main one where Rose slept. If she were really quiet she could creep out without disturbing anyone.

She pulled on her indoor shoes, fleecy trousers and top. Seconds later she was in the hall, then jumped as the letter box rattled and something fell through. She yanked open the door and shone her torchlight into the startled face of Jared Butler.

'Get that light off!' he snarled.

'So it's you!' Caro waved the envelope at him. 'Why are you delivering this missive in the middle of the night, sneaking about other people's property?'

He glared at her.

'Middle of the night? All good folk are up at this hour, minding their own business.'

'This is my business.'

'Is it, now? Fawning round the boss demanding favours? Just leave him alone, will you?'

'You dare to — '

'Watch it, lady. I've got your measure. You're on dangerous ground here. I'm legally allowed on all the estate property, and don't you forget it. I won't have people interfering in the way the place is run, owner or not. Keep your hands off him, d'you hear?'

He turned on his heel and left. The light flickered in Caro's trembling hand as she looked at the writing on the envelope. *The tenant, Hover Cottage.* Across the lawn, vague shapes of trees and bushes were dimly appearing. She shivered and went indoors.

And now there were sounds: a cry from Jonah, and Rose's hurrying footsteps. Her face looked pale in the blazing light in the hall as Caro pressed the switch and Jonah, held in her arms, pressed his face against her shoulder.

'This came for you,' Caro said, handing her the envelope.

They went into the living room and Rose set Jonah down on the floor near his box of toys.

'I'll get us a drink in a minute.'

'Aren't you going to open it?'

'D'you think it's good news? Please, Caro, you do it.'

Still trembling a little, Caro pulled the letter out.

'Shall I read it?'

A quick glance was enough to know that Rose's rent would remain the same until different circumstances transpired. Terse and to the point, but enough to make Rose's face glow with pleasure when Caro read it to her.

'You're a marvel, Caro.'

But Caro didn't feel a marvel. In Jared Butler's first fleeting expression, she had glimpsed a desire for revenge. Here was a man who didn't like being crossed, and would hit out at anyone who got in his way. He was dangerous.

She took the cup of tea that Rose offered, and sipped it, but the fiery liquid did nothing to calm her qualms. The agent's response had been excessive. She had tried and failed to see him yesterday, and instead had confided in the owner, who had thought her explanation reasonable. She had made no accusations against Jared personally. Now Rose would be in the firing line — and after this evening, Caro wouldn't be here to support her.

7

Gentle rain had started to fall by the time breakfast was over, misting the windows and dulling everything outside to gloomy grey.

No car outing today, Caro thought as she carried the empty cereal bowls and milk jug into the kitchen. Rose was wiping the pane of glass in the back door to peer outside, and Jonah squashed in beside her, demanding to look out too.

She picked him up.

'Bubbles?' he said hopefully.

'Raindrops,' she said and then, turning to Caro, 'Tom would have said it's good for the garden, but it doesn't look good out there to me.'

'I've been thinking, Rose,' Caro said abruptly. She picked up the jug to put it in the fridge, then realised it was empty and put it down by the sink again.

'Would you like me to stay on here for a week or two?'

There was no mistaking the pleasure in Rose's sudden smile. 'But aren't you too busy?'

'I could work from here as well as from home, if I planned it carefully. My next assignment is a set of botanical paintings for a book Natasha Gibson is writing. It's a last-minute project as the first artist pulled out. Luckily the publishers thought of me.'

'Natasha Gibson?'

'She's famous in her own field — spring flowers of the hedgerow — so this would be a good place for me to be. I signed the contract a few days ago, and I'm to deliver my work in person to the publisher as soon as I can.'

'In London? But how will you — ?'

'I'll drive to Exeter and leave the car there. I can do it in a day by train.'

Rose put Jonah down, ran water into the sink, and began to wash the dishes at breakneck speed. 'I can't let you do it, Caro. It's too difficult. Could you see to Jonah while I do this? He'll play in the other room.'

There was no more to be said for the moment. Jonah tipped out his toy-box, picked up a brick from the bottom of the pile and looked up at Caro, his eyes bright. She knelt down beside him and kissed the top of his head.

'What are we going to do, Jonah?' she said.

'Big tower. Look!'

'Good decision.'

Caro stretched forward to help Jonah sort out more of the coloured bricks, deep in thought. They had enjoyed their trip to Tavistock yesterday, and Rose had looked less strained as she pushed young Jonah on the swing. He, wanting more, had made them both laugh. Now he placed the last brick on a tottering pile, watched in anticipation until it collapsed, and then gave a shout of joy.

Rose appeared in the doorway, wiping her hands.

'I'd have to go home to Bridport and collect some things,' Caro said before

Rose could open her mouth. 'I could go this afternoon and be back before dark.'

'Caro?' Jonah said. 'Caro's cat.'

Ah yes, Fluffy. She'd forgotten about him for a moment. 'Fluffy shouldn't be a problem.'

Rose was obviously wavering. 'I saw some violets in the hedge the other day . . .'

Caro laughed. 'Does that mean you approve?'

'It would be lovely to have you here.'

'Well then, what's to stop me?'

Rose, laughing, rushed to give her a hug.

★ ★ ★

The tiny ginger-and-white kitten, held lovingly in her neighbour Sandy's hand, was a huge surprise. Surely Fluffy hadn't . . . no, no, of course not. He couldn't have kittens, of course, and she was mad to think so.

'Meet Freddie,' Sandy said proudly. 'Isn't he lovely?'

Stroking the softness of the small head, Caro agreed. 'So where has he come from?'

'My cousin's cat had a surprise litter a few weeks ago, and she rang me yesterday wanting me to have him.' Sandy frowned. 'Fluffy doesn't like him, though. I tried to introduce them but it didn't work. I shut Freddie in our kitchen so he doesn't try to follow me when I go and feed Fluffy, but I can't stay long to give him much attention. I'm glad you've come back, Caro.'

'But not for long,' Caro said. 'I'm planning on spending more time with Rose, and I've come to collect my things. I'd better take Fluffy too.'

'Is that all right?' Sandy looked a little disconcerted. 'OK then, if you're sure. So I'll see you when I see you.'

Caro found Fluffy in the kitchen, looking at her reproachfully. For him to start purring again and rub himself against her legs in a show of affection took some time. Then she made a mug of tea and found some biscuits for herself, before packing a suitcase with the clothes she would need and digging out an old holdall for various other bits and bobs. She didn't forget Fluffy's needs, either. Lastly, she emptied the contents of the fridge into a freezer bag. Her painting gear was all in order; it took only moments to check it was all there, and she was ready to go.

This time, Caro didn't stop at the service station on the way back, but speeded past, anxious not to be away too long. The cavity where her offending tooth had been felt fine now, so there was no need to throw herself on the mercy of a stranger. She had a sudden vision of Liam's blue eyes in his tanned face and the way his hair stuck out over his ears a little, giving him that casual look that made him so attractive. But there was a sharper side to him as well that she had seen when he was speaking on the phone to Jared Butler. Liam was a man of many parts, and she had seen at least three of them. He had proven to be kind and generous when he bought the lilies for Rose, and he had listened with his full attention to her explanation of Mrs Tait's promise to Rose. She'd had every confidence in his tact and sympathy in dealing with the situation. So why had his agent been so obviously furious with him, vowing vengeance on a couple of defenceless women who had done nothing to harm him?

Pondering this, she arrived at the turn-off from the A30 almost before she realised and drove the rest of the way determined to put it to the back of her mind. She parked on the spare ground opposite Hover Cottage and got out. Fluffy, in the cat basket on the back seat, had slept for most of the journey from Bridport but now he gave a soft mew and scrambled to his feet in the small space at his disposal.

'Poor old boy,' she said. 'You've been so good. A few minutes more, and I'll have you out of there and introduced to your hostess and her little boy. He's going to love you.'

The cottage seemed quiet — too quiet. She wondered how she could sense the emptiness even before she had unlatched the front gate. She knew where the key was kept, so there was no trouble getting inside, and she carried Fluffy's basket and litter tray into the kitchen, the best place to let him out and leave him while she got the rest of her gear indoors.

That done, she went to check on him, and then saw the note pinned to the cork board on the wall:

Cindy invited us for tea. Won't be long. Love you. Rose and Jonah XXX

Well, first things first. Caro poured milk into a saucer for Fluffy and plugged in the kettle to make a drink. She carried this into the living room with her mug of tea. Fluffy followed her and then had a good snoop around.

There were sounds outside now . . . the opening of the door, voices, Jonah's

76

high-pitched squeal. Caro drank the rest of her tea and sprang up.

Cindy came marching into the room behind Rose and Jonah and then looked about in suspicion. Her quilted jacket made her look twice her size.

'I can't stay here,' she announced.

'Cat,' said Jonah gleefully, invisible behind the sofa in search of Fluffy. He gave a disappointed wail as the cat shot out and into the kitchen.

'Shut that door!' Cindy ordered and pulled out a handful of tissues from her capacious pocket and mopped her brimming eyes.

Rose, looking bewildered, did as she was told.

This was not a good situation, Caro thought in dismay, as she registered Cindy's alarm. She had known that Rose wouldn't mind her bringing Fluffy back here, and it seemed better than imposing on Sandy for a longer period than usual. But who could have expected this reaction?

'I'm sorry,' she said to Cindy. 'Rose

didn't know Fluffy was coming. It's not her fault.'

But Cindy, sniffing loudly, was gone. The outside door slammed shut so hard the sound reverberated for several seconds.

Rose looked shaken.

'What was all that about?'

'Did you know she's allergic to cats? No, of course you didn't. I'm sorry, Rose, I had to bring him. I feel terrible. Oh, Rose!'

She sank down on the sofa and gazed hopelessly at her. She had wanted to help Rose, and yet she had already made difficulties by bringing Fluffy back with her. The false impression Cindy had gained from Liam's joking remark on their first meeting didn't help, either. There was nothing for it but to try and make her peace with her.

'I'll have to do something — '

'Could you take her some flowers, d'you think?'

Caro frowned, considering.

Rose looked about for inspiration.

'Chocolate, then. She loves chocolates.'

'Chocolate?' said Jonah with interest. His mother leaned forward and gave him a hug as he crawled out from his hiding place.

'Tomorrow,' Caro said. 'We'll take a walk up to the village, shall we, and see what we can get in the village store? And then when we come back, we'll take Fluffy out into the garden so he can have a good look out there. Then I'll leave you two eating chocolate and head off for the Manor. How does that sound?'

'Perfect,' said Rose. 'Will Fluffy be all right out there in the kitchen by himself while I help you sort out your things?'

'Lucky to be there, all things considered,' Caro said with feeling.

'He's always welcome,' said Rose stoutly. 'Just like you are, Caro.'

Caro stood up. She was so lucky to have them, Rose and Jonah. Fortunate too to have the opportunity to be useful to Rose when she needed her, and to be welcome in her home.

8

Caro's heart was thumping in apprehension the nearer she got to Hovercombe Manor, all the more so from having had forty-eight hours to think about it.

Rose had assured her that Cindy could be reached if she rang the bell on the door at the far side of the building that she used as her private entrance. No chance of running into Liam then and that was good. He had seen her at a disadvantage before and the memory of that still rankled.

Cindy answered the doorbell at once. 'It's you!'

She looked suspiciously at the parcel wrapped in flowery paper that Caro held out to her.

'What's this?'

'It's a peace offering, Cindy. Chocolates. I hope you like them. I hope you're feeling better now. I'm truly sorry about my cat.'

Cindy rubbed her hands down the side of her jeans. Frowning, she took the proffered gift.

'You'd best come in.'

A kettle was bubbling away on the Aga and on the table in the centre of the room stood a blue glazed vase brimming with daffodils.

Caro exclaimed in pleasure as she sat down and leaned forward to finger one of the petals, admiring the translucent paleness tinged with brighter yellow.

'They're beautiful. You love flowers?'

Cindy made coffee in thick multi-coloured mugs, and pushed one in Caro's direction alongside a plate of biscuits. 'Doesn't everyone?

Caro smiled. 'I'd like to think so. It's my job, you see, painting flowers. I've been asked to do some botanical paint-ings to illustrate a book. That's what I'm trying to work on at the moment.'

'At Rose's place?'

'I wasn't planning to move into the

manor house.' Caro held her breath and then let out a sigh of relief as a slight smile lightened Cindy's grim expression.

'Mr Tait loves his little joke, but he soon put me right. You'd come to see him on business.'

'I wanted to see the agent, but he wasn't here.'

'Jared Butler, the slimy toad.'

'You don't like him?'

Cindy bit into a biscuit and then finished the rest with a gulp. 'No one does. So what's botanical painting?'

'I'll show you some of my work if you like. I've made a start on some of the wild flowers near Rose's place. Oh, no . . . you can't come over, can you, because of Fluffy? I'm so sorry, Cindy.'

'Not your fault,' Cindy said gruffly.

Caro took another biscuit. 'May I? These are good. Did you make them?'

'Mr Tait's favourite.'

'And great coffee too. Thank you. I'll bring some of my paintings here to show you, if you like? Not yet. It's slow work, you see, and I'm still on the first. I sneaked a wild primrose from the bank in the lane, but don't tell anyone or I might end up in jail.'

'I doubt Mr Tait would issue a summons anyway. Pick some daffs on the way out, why don't you? I'd come with you, but I've a meal to get into the slow cooker for when he gets back.'

This seemed like a signal for Caro to go, and she took it. She left her car where it was and walked across the lawn to where a mass of daffodils bloomed by a low, lichen-covered wall. Such a variety of shades, from deep cadmium yellow to pure white. Some were multi-headed, others had trumpets of orange and gold. Their heady perfume hung on the air. She gazed, entranced, and didn't hear the soft footfall approaching until Liam spoke.

'You like them?'

'They're stunning.'

'Aren't they just?'

Liam's eyes looked deep blue because of his shirt of the same colour.

It seemed not to matter that she was contemplating picking some of his flowers and carrying them away with her. He didn't question why she was here, and she offered no explanation.

'I was on my way to the walled garden,' he said, 'to inspect Kevin's improvements and to hear about the gardening couple he's been interviewing on my behalf. We'll need more staff if our plans go ahead. Like to take a look?'

Going with him seemed the most natural thing in the world, and so was hearing about the ideas that his head gardener, Kevin, bandied about between them. The only surprise was that Jared Butler wasn't here thinking up ways to jeopardise anything he didn't agree with. But that was her imagination going into overdrive. Caro listened to the two of them, smiling.

The walled garden looked larger now that some of the ramshackle sheds had been removed. There were extra raised beds too, planted with rows of primulas and velvet wallflowers. At the entrance was a large paved area that had obviously been laid recently. Liam looked at it with interest, nodding his head and congratulating Kevin on his speedy work that had resulted in the proposed opening of the nursery garden being ahead of schedule.

'We're planning an extension to the existing building,' he said, turning to Caro. 'Much bigger and lighter for the sales area.' He indicated a door in the far wall. 'That hasn't been opened for years, but Kevin's had a go at it. It leads almost directly into the orangery, and I have plans for that too. Come. I'll show you.'

His face shone with an enthusiasm that she found contagious.

The orangery was a large airy room on the south side of the house, the glass in its walls and ceiling sparkling in the sunlight. The tiled floor had been recently washed and there were still damp places beneath the slatted wooden shelves at the sides of the room where the sunshine didn't quite reach.

'Don't tell me,' she said. 'A café, a place for people to come for refreshment after buying in the walled garden?'

His quick smile showed his approval.

'Got it in one. Clever girl. Trailing plants on the shelves, carved metal tables and chairs.'

'I can smell the coffee now, and see the arrays of delicious pastries. Devon Cream Teas too? My mouth's watering.'

'It'll be good for Cindy. Give her something to do.'

'Apart from running the house, of course, making sure everything's ticking over smoothly?'

'That too.'

He sounded perfectly serious but there was a smile in his voice.

'She's a worker, our Cindy,' he said. 'I found that out soon enough. I think she feels life's a bit dull now with me away so much.'

'I had coffee with her just now. She didn't mention any of this.'

He tapped the side of his nose. 'Sworn to secrecy, that's why.'

'Then I'm flattered to have been shown around.'

'You think it will work?'

She had no doubt of that. She had the feeling that everything he set his mind to would be successful.

'It's useful as a short-term project, anyway,' he said. 'We'll see how it goes. I have plans to open the gardens to the public one day, too.'

'As well as your landscape gardening commitments?'

'We'll need more staff, of course. Boost the local employment. That can't be bad, can it?'

She agreed, of course, and told him so; and as they walked back to where she had left her car, he expounded on more of his ideas.

'But they're on hold for the time being,' he said with a smile. 'I shall be away for a while now — a huge commitment that needs my full attention.'

She wondered what it was but didn't ask. Time was flying and she had promised Rose she wouldn't be long. There was her work to consider too.

Only when she was unlatching the garden gate at the cottage did she remember that she hadn't picked any of the daffodils to bring with her. Her mind had been on other things, like Liam's imminent departure. She hadn't felt anything at all like this since she and Rob had split up, and had vowed she never would again. But this man had somehow got under her defences, and she didn't know how that had happened.

9

Caro gazed down at the head of the dog violet she had placed on the pad of cotton wool in a saucer of water. This was to maintain its freshness, and to provide a close-up view of the specimen as she set to work. Her painting was going well in all its intricate detail, but after hours of this she was exhausted. She laid down her brush, stood up and stretched. Outside, the sun was shining; Rose had taken Jonah up to the village, and planned to call on Cindy on the way back.

Caro's sense of freedom had meant she had settled down to work with an easy mind. Even Fluffy was entertaining himself out there on the lawn, chasing the odd sparrow but never catching it. He had settled in surprisingly well, as if he had been living here all his life. It was good to see. So, an hour or two to herself to work at a pace she found restful was an unaccustomed luxury. Even though the rickety table was small and the space around her limited, she felt her usual contentment at losing herself in the bloom in front of her. She sat down again and, picking up her brush, dipped the tip in the violet paint on the palette.

Suddenly a blaring car horn and screech of brakes outside startled her into jumping up and rushing to the window, heart thudding. She could see nothing of the lane from here but something had happened. Moments later, she was outside, and saw at once that a vehicle was slewed across the lane and that there was no sign of Fluffy. She reached the gate in time as the driver emerged from the car, rubbing his hand across his forehead and looking slightly dazed.

'Are you hurt?'

'No thanks to that damn cat.'

'Fluffy?'

It wasn't hard to work out what had

happened, but Caro took a moment to register that the man was Jared Butler. She had seen him angry before, but this time his sudden burst of rage was incandescent.

'I'm sorry — '

'I could have been killed.'

Or Fluffy could have been obliterated as he dashed across the lane. Her instant thought was hurriedly repressed. The man was in shock, and no wonder. To ask if he had been driving too fast for the slight bend in the lane would not be appropriate at this moment.

Meekly, she took the stream of abuse that followed, but moved back a little in case he had any thoughts of physical attack. At last he gave up, got into his vehicle, and slammed shut the door.

'You haven't heard the last of this,' he snarled through the open window. 'Look at the contract. Legal, this time, and I'll see it's carried out. Backdated.'

The loathing in the last word was stunning.

His engine roared. He yanked the

steering wheel around and headed off in the direction of Bradfield Farm further down the lane.

Caro stood quite still, staring after him. If he was suffering from shock then so was she, largely from the invective that poured from him. At last she gave herself a shake and looked around for the offending Fluffy. Nowhere to be seen, of course, and hopefully hiding somewhere to lick his metaphorical wounds in peace.

She went indoors, and to her dismay found a smudge across her precious illustration where her brush had fallen as she rushed out. Her morning's work was wasted, and Rose and Jonah would be back soon. And once more Fluffy was in trouble — his own fault this time, and likely to have serious repercussions if Jared Butler's insinuations could be believed.

The arrival of Rose and Jonah at the moment — accompanied by the offending Fluffy — was a distraction and a relief.

'We met him in the lane,' Rose said.

Caro bent to stroke him and check for possible injuries. There were none as far as she could tell. Rose's eyes looked brighter than they had for days and her cheeks were slightly flushed. Jonah, too, clutching a bag of something, looked happy. The daffodils that Rose was carrying brightened the slight dimness in the room, but their subtle scent was submerged in the joyful perfume of the lilies.

'Cindy made some special sweets for Jonah,' Rose said. 'He's a lucky boy, but he's not to start on them until after his lunch.'

Jonah, interested now only in Fluffy, relinquished the bag willingly.

Rose sniffed at her flowers. 'I'll get these in water, and then I'd better get started on something to eat as we're a bit late.'

'But not for a moment,' Caro said. 'There's something that needs doing first.'

Rose looked at her, her head held a

little to one side. 'Is something wrong, Caro? You sound serious.'

'Is your rental contract handy, Rose? We need to take a look at it.'

Rose didn't ask why but went to unearth it, taking the daffodils with her. Moments later she had spread the document out on the hearthrug where they could both read it.

'Are we looking for something special?' Rose asked, kneeling at Caro's side.

Only then did Caro tell her of her fears for Fluffy.

'Don't worry, Caro,' Rose said. 'I know we're allowed to keep pets, so Fluffy's here perfectly legally. He's not going to be thrown out.'

But remembering the agent's parting shot, Caro couldn't quite believe it. As Rose got up to see to lunch she continued to look at each clause carefully. It didn't take long.

She folded the paper and got to her feet too. 'Where d'you keep it, Rose? Better put it away safely.'

Rose took the paper from her. 'It lives in the bottom drawer in our bedroom. My bedroom, I mean. Fluffy's allowed to stay, is he?'

'Yes, Fluffy's quite safe. He won't be evicted if he can't pay his rent.'

Rose, laughing, continued with her preparations, and Caro went to help her. Deep in thought, she carried the dishes to the dining table, and when all was ready lifted Jonah into his high-chair. Although her contribution to the household expenses was a generous one, it probably wasn't enough to cover the increase in rent as well. The last paragraph in the contract had made it quite clear that tenants could not take lodgers without a rent increase being enforced. Rose, of course, didn't consider her a lodger — but that, if she stayed longer, was effectively what she was.

And now, because of Fluffy, Jared Butler was well aware of that fact.

★ ★ ★

95

'I'm thinking of taking off for a while on my own,' Caro said as she helped clear away and wash up. Jonah, eyes bleary with sleep, had been carried off to his bed ten minutes ago.

Rose handed her the last glass to be dried and put away.

'Where will you go?'

She sounded perfectly content to be staying at home. She had been making progress in travelling by car, but mustn't be hurried.

'Dartmoor, I thought. Not too far. I might head for that tor I was reading about in the book on my beside table.'

'Brentor? That's the one with the church on the top. You can see it from miles around.'

Caro glanced out of the window. The sky was as clear as it had been this morning when Jared Butler had burst upon the scene. Up there on Brentor, she would see clearly, just as she hoped to see the way forward for both Rose and herself in the future. She needed space and time on her own to do that, and this was a good way to get it.

She set out soon afterwards, supplied with the flask of tea that Rose had insisted she take. 'It might be cold up there,' she'd said. 'And you'll be tired from climbing up to it from the car park.'

With the help of the Ordnance Survey map Rose lent her, and being able to spot her destination every time the lane twisted in a certain direction, Caro found the place easily enough. She set off up the steep path, aware of the scent of crushed grass and the peaty aroma of bare earth. It was certainly an impressive sight, those jagged rocks on their crag high above her, and perched on top of them this perfect little church that seemed to have been there for ever.

The view of moor and field in every direction was magnificent. She sank down on the nearest rocky outcrop at the top to take it in and to consider this latest problem Jared had sprung on her. *Look at the contract*, he had said, knowing full well she would learn of the clause that gave him the power to increase the rent of Hover Cottage to a sum Rose could ill afford.

The obvious thing was for her to return her own home — but how could she do that now when Jared Butler's bullying ways could make Rose's life a misery? And there was something else too, a reason she hardly dared admit even to herself: the thought of seeing Liam Tait only rarely was strangely disturbing.

She could, of course, decide to stay, and work even harder to raise the extra money. She could attend craft fairs and markets in the hope of selling her paintings. She could research suitable outlets in the towns roundabout, and perhaps teach at evening classes. But that wouldn't really work even if it were possible, because she would be away from Hover Cottage for long periods, and that wouldn't be good for Rose or for the fulfilling the commissions she had on hand.

Or — and this was the big one — she could put her house on the market, and find something smaller and cheaper to purchase locally. This would free up money to help Rose. It would be more difficult to access London, of course, and more expensive. She loved her home area, but this was good too.

Dartmoor was at its best on a day like this, but little help to her now in her decision-making. She stood up and went into the church through the squeaking gate that guarded the porch. The door clanged behind her, echoing through the shadowy building. She thought of the three myths she had read of how the church had come to be built on this extraordinary spot. In one, it was said that the devil raised a fierce storm in Plymouth Sound that blew out the beacon light on the tor and resulted in a rich merchant ship heading for rocks. There followed a fierce battle of wills between them, that the merchant won and he built the church as a thanks offering. Another myth involved a settlement at the base of the tor long ago in the mists of time. The inhabitants decided to build themselves a church. To their dismay, the devil had other ideas, and when it was finished they woke one morning to find the building gone. They resolved to try again next day but discovered that the devil had put the church back, not at the bottom but perched high on the tor above them. Caro smiled. Well, the building was still here today — and used, she read in one of the pamphlets, on important occasions throughout the church year.

One or two others had entered the building now and were admiring the loving care bestowed on it over a vast period of time. The stained-glass window above the altar made a beautiful splash of colour. As she wandered around, Caro wondered about yet another myth, this time that the rich merchant feared for his life and the fate of the crew in the violent storm that blew up out of nowhere. He vowed that if they could be safely delivered to shore, he would build a church on the first land he saw. His prayers were answered, and he built the church on the top of Brentor. Mmm, that sounded more likely, and was the one that she would go for.

Outside in the sunshine again she found her previous seat, seated herself as comfortably as she could, and unscrewed the top of her flask.

A couple passing by smiled at her.

'A glorious day, isn't it?'

'Lovely.'

They stopped for a moment and the woman looked into the distance, shading her eyes with one hand.

'And it's so clear we can see for miles in every direction. Can you see Brown Willy over there in the west? That's Cornwall's highest peak on Bodmin Moor. And to the north-east is Exmoor, a good forty miles from here. It's brilliant, isn't it, all this space? It clears your head, somehow.'

Her companion indicated Caro's

thermos and smiled as they began to move off.

'You're being sensible.'

Caro smiled too. Rose, bless her. And she must be sensible too. What was holding her back from relocating? Her need to be single-minded meant little time for socialising, and apart from Sandy next door, there was no one who would miss her much — or even notice she wasn't there. Sad, of course, but something she had to live with if she wanted to be successful in her chosen career. It would be the same here, except that Rose would welcome her, and so would Jonah in his own inimitable way. Only this morning he had toddled into her bedroom, smiled his beaming smile, before beating a hasty retreat. Looking for Fluffy, she supposed.

She drank her tea and packed the flask away in her bag. As soon as she got back, she would phone Sandy — or, better still, why not now? She needed to discuss this with someone, and who was better than a friend who would give an impartial judgement before she put her plan into action?

10

The belt of rain that followed Caro to Dorset two days later seemed to hover over Bridport all the time she was there. Even her house seemed damp, and there was air of gloom over everything. Sandy, though, greeted her with a broad smile that showed her delight in the decision Caro had made.

'It's not that I'm not sorry that you'll be leaving us,' she said. 'Don't get me wrong, Caro. I'll miss you tons.'

Caro smiled as she returned her hug. 'I'll miss you too, Sandy. You've been a good neighbour.'

'Let's hope I'll be a good neighbour to Bob's mum from now on. I still can't believe Bob and I are buying you out with her massive help. We'll be able to connect the two quite easily, being semi-detached. He's over the moon . . . ' Sandy broke off, obviously overcome.

They were in Sandy's kitchen and at their feet her new kitten played with some rolled-up newspaper he was treating like a hated enemy. Fluffy had been like that once all those years ago when she had first come to live here, Caro thought. Now he was settling into Hover Cottage as if it had been his home right from the start. Somehow it seemed like betrayal.

She sniffed and blew her nose.

'But Caro, you're absolutely sure of this?' Sandy looked at her anxiously. 'You wouldn't like more time to think about it?'

Caro shook her head.

'I'm absolutely sure. I know it's the right thing to do, only — '

'I know, I know. They say that next to bereavement, moving house causes the most stress.'

'But not with me.' Caro reached for Sandy's hand and pressed it. 'Not when I know it's you who'll be living in it.'

'And you'll come back sometimes to see us? There will always be room for you to stay as long as you like.'

Caro laughed rather shakily.

'I can't promise to say the same thing to you at the moment. Rose's place would bulge at the seams. But as soon as I've got somewhere of my own, you'll be my first visitors, you and Bob. And I hope that time will come very soon.'

She had made an appointment to see her solicitor this afternoon, after she had been to an independent firm to arrange a valuation. She and her neighbours had already come to an agreement, but she thought it sensible to check with a professional that it was a reasonable one in the present market. Now she needed to start on some clearing-up, especially outside. But not today. She glanced at the window. Outside, the rain was still streaming down, and the sky looked black.

'I'd better get back to my place,' she said, pushing her chair back as she stood up. 'Masses to do.'

She would take with her another suitcase or two, plus a few other odds and ends, and return for more in due course. Sandy and Bob had already told her their plans for converting the ground floor of her place into a granny flat for his elderly and infirm mother. With help from her financially, this was possible, and would suit them all. Everything was in place and likely to work well as long as the sale went through as quickly as could be managed under the present-day requirements of buying and selling.

* * *

At Hover Cottage, Caro found Rose in the kitchen preparing lunch. She shut the fridge door so hard it sprang open again.

'I put Jonah down late for his rest,' Rose said when she had closed it again and welcomed Caro with a hug. 'We'll be able to eat in peace. And what d'you think, Caro? I've got some news for you.'

'You have?'

'Something you'll like.'

'Oh?' Jared Butler being sent away for good? Too much to hope for, surely. But miracles sometimes happened.

'We've been invited to a house-warming party at the Manor on Saturday, a party for the tenants. What d'you think of that?'

Caro frowned. 'Tenants?'

'That means you too, Caro.'

Rose was looking at her expectantly, but Caro was worried. If she was regarded as a tenant, then that meant Rose's rent would soon be raised, and that was definitely not good news. She tried to smile.

'And have you accepted for both of us?'

'Of course. Straight away. He said he wouldn't leave until I did.'

'Liam Tait?' Caro's heart seemed to miss a beat.

'He's delivering all the invitations

personally. He came here first just after breakfast. He's such a nice man, just like you said, Caro. I wish you'd been here.'

Caro did, too. She turned away to hide her confusion.

'I've got a load of stuff to bring in,' she said, 'but it can wait till later. Come into the other room, Rose, and hear what I have to say.'

'About the party?'

'Something better.'

All eagerness, Rose did as she was told. She sat down in the chair near the stove and pushed Jonah's stool away with her foot.

'How would you like it if I came and lived somewhere near you permanently?'

Rose looked bewildered. 'I don't see — '

'I've made arrangements to sell my house. Sandy and Bob are going to buy it.'

'But — '

'It's all arranged.'

Rose's face looked blank. 'But you can't do that.'

'I've already done it.'

'But why? Your house is so roomy, and so convenient for everything.'

'That's exactly the point. Having it helped get me started on something I really wanted that makes me feel fulfilled — happy, even. But you should have had some of that money from Aunt Maggie, Rose.'

'But where will you live?'

Caro shrugged. 'I'm hoping you won't throw me out until I've found somewhere.'

'As if.'

'But there's still a problem in the meantime, and I blame Fluffy. Because of the wretched animal shooting across the lane at the wrong moment, Bully Butler knows I'm here, and will do his worst.'

Rose gave a little giggle. 'Fluffy's a cat. Cats do that sort of thing.'

Caro felt her face muscles relax as she smiled too.

'I need to pay the extra rent while I'm living with you, and until the house is sold, it'll be difficult.'

'I'll get a job to pay the extra rent,' Rose said.

'We've been through this — '

'That's the other thing I was going to tell you. There's a part-time one coming up, you see. Cindy told me about it. I've got to go and see about it next Tuesday, but I don't know — '

'And what is it, this job?'

'It's at the garden centre — a nursery garden, really.'

'A nursery garden? At the Manor?'

Rose's bright look faded. 'It's a job.'

Caro was sorry for her implied criticism. Of course it was a job, and an interesting one for anyone keen on plants. But when had Rose ever been that? As a girl, she hadn't even known the difference between a buttercup and a celandine, and probably didn't even now.

'So we'll have a garden expert on our hands?' she said.

'The thing is — '

'Yes?'

'Will I be any good?'

Caro took a deep breath. She had come to learn how to deal with this lack of confidence, and now she said, 'Of course not. Whatever gave you that idea?'

Rose looked at her uncertainly. 'You're teasing me?'

Caro made her tone deliberately light. 'Would I do a thing like that?'

'And you approve?'

'Why not?'

'But . . . there's Jonah.'

Ah yes, Jonah. Obviously there was no one local who was free to look after him. Or no one whom Rose felt she could trust.

'I'll be here to look after Jonah.' Caro tried not to sound the least discouraging. A helping hand was what Rose needed, and who was she to start making difficulties? Someone who cared for her and didn't want to see her get hurt, that's who.

She got to her feet and walked across to the window. Outside, the wind was shaking the tops of the trees: she saw on the lower branches of the sycamore that the swollen buds were beginning to break, and one was in almost full leaf. All of a sudden she wanted to paint it, to capture the joyousness of it as it swayed there in the rising breeze.

'Caro?'

She spun around to see Rose looking at her with a questioning expression in her eyes.

'You really think it's a good idea?'

'Of course I do.' She wanted Rose to stand on her own two feet, but it was strangely unsettling. Rose had decided to do something for herself, and yet she was still-dependent on her to help out by babysitting Jonah. Two-year-olds were active, learning to make sense of their environment and discovering all sorts of interesting new activities. She loved him dearly, but giving him all the attention he needed was going to be exhausting, and would leave little time

113

to concentrate on her own work. But if that was the price she had to pay for doing her best for Rose in the interim, then so be it.

'I haven't got the job yet,' Rose said doubtfully.

'There's the party for you to look forward to first.'

Rose brightened. 'And for you, Caro.'

Caro sprang up.

'Come on then, girl. Action. We're not beaten yet. Bully Butler, look out! I'll work hard this afternoon, and for the next few days too. The sooner those illustrations are done, the better, and I'll have time to take them up to London before our Working Woman gets going. Yes?'

Rose giggled again.

'You're good for me, Caro. Did you know that?'

'That's what I'm here for.'

Caro felt a glow inside now, a feeling that in a few weeks everything would be fine. In the short term, there was the tenants' party at the Manor, and Liam had made a special request for her to be there. She might be doing her best for Rose by making a few sacrifices on her part, but at the same time there was the warm feeling of being sought after by someone whom she now realised was beginning to mean a great deal to her.

11

At lunchtime on Saturday the Orangery at Hovercombe Manor was unrecognisable with its festoons of greenery hanging from the narrow wooden slats in the glass roof. Caro gazed at the transformation in wonder. Rose, too, holding Jonah by the hand, was admiring the banks of camellias that brightened each corner in all their colourful glory.

Liam stepped forward through a throng of people. He had flattened his dark hair a little today, but Caro could see that at any moment it was going to spring back into its usual unique style. She longed to run her fingers through it . . . but what was she thinking of? A good thing that thought had stayed inside her head, and she hadn't blurted it out loud. She smiled.

'I'd introduce you,' he said, 'but you

can see how it is.' He stooped to pat Jonah's head. 'Hello, young fellow.' And then to Rose, 'He might like to play with the other children outside, but maybe he's a little too young?'

'Well, yes . . . ' Rose spoke doubtfully. 'Would you like that, Jonah?'

The little boy looked up at Liam, wide-eyed, and clung fast to his mother's skirt.

Liam gave him a beaming smile. 'Perhaps not, then.'

Caro glanced outside through the glass wall of the Orangery. On the terrace, children of varying sizes were amusing themselves with some large quoits. Then, tiring of this, they ran down onto the lawn, laughing and shouting.

'They get on well together,' she said.

'They live on neighbouring farms,' Liam told her. 'There are older children too — adults now, most of them — but they're all inside. And there's Evie over there alone, sitting on the wall. She's fifteen or so. The Barnets live at

Bradfield Farm. Come and get a drink, you two. Food, too. Cindy and her mother have done us proud. It's through there, in the dining room.'

He gave then an encouraging smile and then moved off to greet some newcomers.

Rose was looking rather lost now, and Jonah, still clinging to her, about to cry.

'Follow me,' Caro said.

The crush eased a little as they entered the dining room where Cindy and an older woman were presiding over a table so laden with goodies that Caro wondered it didn't collapse under the strain.

Rose was being greeted now in a friendly manner, and Jonah being made much of.

'I'll see you outside, Rose,' Caro said.

She was beginning to feel in the way, a stranger among all these farming people who had so much to say to each other. The rising noise was getting to her, too. A breath of fresh air would be good.

There was no sign of the girl Evie, or the younger children now, and for a few moments Caro was alone with her plate of food and the glass of fruit punch she had picked up on her way out. The muted sounds from the building behind her were pleasant from here, and the fresh spring air was welcome. She found a bench against one wall where it was sheltered and sat down on it to eat.

A few others filtered out, as pleased as she was to be in the open air. Among them was Rose, carrying a plate of food in one hand and holding Jonah by the other. She sat down beside Caro with a breath of relief and lifted Jonah up to sit beside them.

'I can't see Jared Butler anywhere about,' she said.

'You're not worried about meeting him here?'

Rose shook her head. 'Not really, but — '

'No buts,' Caro said firmly. 'We're invited guests, Rose. He's not going to attack you here.'

'I suppose not.'

Rose had tied a napkin round Jonah's neck and given him a large sausage roll. Bemused, the little boy took a huge bite.

'D'you think I could have a look at the vegetable garden?' Rose said when they had cleared their plates. 'That's where I'll be working if I get the job.'

Caro nodded. 'Good idea. I'll come with you. We'll let the crowd inside thin a little before we tackle the desserts.'

The gate into the walled garden was stiff, but Caro gave it a good push and they were inside. Only a week or two had passed since Liam had given her the guided tour, but already she could see changes in the beds, now showing signs that this was serious business. In one of the greenhouses there were neat rows of young plants already doing well. Stacks of seed trays were piled outside the new building too.

Rose looked at them in dismay.

'What are they for?'

'For planting more seeds,' Caro told her. 'When the seedlings are big enough, they'll be transplanted into smaller trays, ready for selling. That might be your job.'

Rose gulped.

'But I won't know what to do.'

'Kevin will show you, Rose. You'll be fine.'

Rose didn't look convinced. The sound of footsteps made her glance behind her. Caro looked up too and saw Liam approaching, looking relaxed in his chinos and blue shirt. His wristwatch caught a flicker of sunshine as he moved his arm.

'I wondered where you were,' he said.

He seemed unsurprised at finding them here. Caro supposed that, as his tenants had been invited to the Manor, they were free to roam where they chose. If it happened to be in the vegetable garden, then who was he to comment? She smiled at her ability to work this out.

Rose looked apologetic.

'I've applied for a job here, you see,' she said. 'I'm coming on Tuesday to see about it.'

'And I'm trying to convince her that she can do it.' Caro added.

'Caro knows about plants and flowers.'

Liam looked at her, his head a little to one side and amusement in his eyes. 'We have an expert here?'

'Caro's good at everything,' Rose said.

'Oh?'

Caro felt herself flush at the wealth of meaning in that word. Was he remembering the fuss she had made over some almost non-existent blood? She hurried to explain that Rose had wanted to see what was involved, and it had seemed a good time to do it.

'Of course,' he said smoothly. 'Have you seen enough now?'

'Oh yes.' Rose gave a heavy emphasis on her answer, and then seemed to realise how it sounded. 'Thank you,' she added politely.

Jonah had seemed awed to see Liam at first, but now he tried to pull away. Caro held tightly to his hand.

'I think he's needing more food. Some of that ice-cream — '

'Ice-cream,' Jonah said. 'Cake, Mummy.'

Liam smiled. 'Plenty of that there, if I know our Cindy.'

He walked back with them, leaving them at the door of the dining room. Caro didn't see him after that, but the warm feeling of his presence stayed with her as they chose from the delicious spread in front of them and returned to the terrace.

She finished her tarte au citron and leaned back dreamily against the warm wall. Others were standing about, talking and eating, and among them she caught site of the girl, Evie, still sitting some way apart and looking as if she would like some food but was too shy to do anything about it. A ridiculous thought, perhaps, but on impulse Caro got up to make sure.

'You're not eating?' she said.

'No, I — '

'Too big a crowd in there? It's thinned out now, though. Shall we go in together?'

Evie got up obediently, shaking back her long straight hair, and followed Caro inside.

'Are you here on your own?' Caro said as she ushered her towards the table.

'Mum and Dad couldn't come. My brothers are here somewhere.' She looked round vaguely.

Caro smiled. 'I see. Then let's make up for it now. I'm new here, and I don't know many people, but I know the food is delicious.'

The people at the table moved away — and standing there, looking in her direction, was Jared Butler.

'Ah,' he said, in a voice full of menace.

'It's a good party.'

'Very good. A party for the tenants of Hovercombe Manor Estate.'

'To give it its full title,' she agreed.

'So why are you here if you're not a tenant? The tenants' party, and you're here in the thick of it. In my book, that proves you're a tenant too.'

The malevolent expression on his face seemed to deepen. Caro hesitated for one moment. The she pulled herself to her full height and looked him straight in the eye.

'I'm not a tenant; I'm an invited guest.' She let a beat fall. 'Unlike you, I suspect.'

A roar of scornful laughter from the nearby group seemed to shake the room.

'Well done, lass!'

'A good try, Jared.'

'Got you there, lad!'

'Clear off, why don't you? Get yourself home where you belong.'

Jared's face reddened. The voices seemed to echo in Caro's head as he slunk off. All at once, she felt dizzy with the enormity of what she had said, and all for a childish wish to get the better of him. As the seemingly self-appointed champion of people who disliked him as much as she, did a polite reply would have been the sensible option. Who was she, a stranger, to confront the agent and manager, even though he clearly had it in for her — and, through her, for Rose?

She was no longer hungry. Evie had filled a plate, and was with a young man who was obviously her brother. Caro would like to have slunk off home too, but there were Rose and Jonah to consider. She rubbed her hand across her eyes and felt herself sway.

'Come with me.' A voice — a strong voice, and one with authority. 'Look after things here, Mum.'

Caro felt herself propelled through a doorway and into a room that was blessedly quiet and cool. The next moment, she was sitting on a sofa with Cindy beside her, an anxious expression on her broad face.

'Take no notice of that devious toad,' she said. 'A hot drink is what you want. Stay here.'

Caro wasn't about to do anything else. Her limbs felt heavy and her mind a fuzzy mass of regret and embarrassment. Her words to Jared had slipped out so easily. It had been instinctive on her part because of his greeting to her, but she should have stopped to think. She had believed that she had the measure of the man, and had expected a sharp retort or two, but not this surprising reaction. There was something going on here that she couldn't understand . . . but how was she to know that the bystanders would have shown her their support in so enthusiastic a manner, and given it a great deal more importance than it otherwise might have had?

Cindy seemed to want no apologies, or even excuses. 'He had it coming to him. I saw the expression on his face, and others did too.'

'I made a fool of him in front of a lot of people,' Caro said as she accepted the mug of tea Cindy handed to her.

'Don't you fear for him. He made a fool of himself, and we were all glad to see it.'

'What will he do now?'

Cindy shrugged.

'Who cares? Convince himself that he was doing his duty, I expect. He's the only one round here who thinks he's doing that, I can tell you. You've no need to worry.'

'It's Rose I'm worried about. He bullies her. That's why I'm here. If I'm around, I can look out for her.'

Cindy looked so sympathetic as she sat there in her too-thick jersey, taking up more than half of the sofa, that Caro found herself confiding in her. Cindy was a good ally, a good person to have on her side. A good friend. Her ferocious tirade against the agent who had started throwing his weight around was exactly what Caro wanted to hear.

She took a sip of tea and then almost choked.

'It's sweet.'

'Two spoonfuls of sugar.'

'But I don't take sugar.'

'You do today. Good for shock, they say.'

'But I'm not shocked. I feel great talking to you.'

'It's the sugar, not me talking. Drink up.'

'No way.'

Cindy's eyes sparkled. It was clear she appreciated someone with a will of her own. Caro got to her feet.

'I shall pour this away and help myself to more.'

'You do that.'

Her friendly tone of voice was invigorating. Caro smiled. Cindy approved of her, and some good had come out of bad. Great and double great!

She was aware of music now, and a sudden quietness inside the house.

'That's Ryan on his violin,' Cindy said as she struggled to her feet and picked up the tray. 'A dab hand at it, he is. Wandering about the garden, I expect, the show-off. The children'll be out there too, on the Treasure Hunt. Bags going on.'

And so Caro found when she went outside again, looking for Rose and Jonah. Music was playing somewhere out of sight, and it sounded as if there was more than one instrument. Another violin, perhaps; a clarinet? She couldn't quite tell, but the effect was pleasing. People were wandering about the lawns, glasses in hand, making the most of the sunshine. Even the breeze had dropped and there was an air of enjoyment about the place that was catching. She was glad to see Rose and Jonah down there in the distance.

Caro turned to find Liam beside her.

12

'Enjoying yourself, Caro?'

She hesitated.

' Something wrong?'

'Not with this lovely party.'

'But you're not joining in? A walk about the place to admire the azaleas? Vegetables springing up in the walled garden?'

'You think of everything,' she said, smiling.

'But not for you?'

He looked so concerned, it would have been easy to tell him of her encounter with Jared Butler if she hadn't felt so embarrassed. Jared's malicious expression had been frightening the moment before he'd moved off and disappeared. She shuddered now to think of it.

'I feel like a little time on my own.' And that was the wrong thing to say, too. She should have brought a roll of sticky tape and used it to good effect on her mouth.

'I know the feeling.'

'You do?'

'Occasionally.' He took a deep breath and gazed round at the spacious lawns where his guests were happily wandering.

'You have a lovely place here.'

'Too well-laid-out for my purpose, I fear. I envisaged the chance to start afresh with my own students on residential courses throughout the year, and use the place to try out their own landscaping ideas. I think there would be a riot locally if I got the diggers in to tear all this up, don't you? And the house is a home, not a place that be easily converted to take students.'

'You have big ideas.'

'And dreams.' He grinned. 'How ridiculous all that sounds.'

'It's good to have dreams,' she said.

'And you need time on your own too, you said, so why don't we escape together?'

'Now?'

He waved his arm around to indicate the grass, the shrubbery, the house. His guests seemed to be enjoying themselves. She could see young Evie on the terrace, with her brother and two others, balancing a quoit on her head like a crown and laughing as it fell off.

'I'm the genial host, remember?'

His smile was so warm she felt her guilt fade away. Her words to the agent had been simple enough. Anyone else would have laughed them off; but Jared had taken them badly. They had obviously hit home, for whatever reason. But that was his problem; she was here in Liam's territory as an invited guest, and he had sought her out to make sure she was enjoying herself. A perfect host, in fact.

He was looking serious now.

'I was thinking,' he said, 'of a place on Dartmoor that might appeal to you as an artist. I'd like to take you there. I have a client to see near Moretonhampstead on Tuesday morning, and I thought you might be interested in visiting Mulvery Court afterwards too?'

Astonished, she gazed at him.

'You don't like the idea?'

'Well, yes — ' She felt stupidly tongue-tied. She was a woman of nearly thirty, for goodness' sake, not a teenager invited out on her first date.

She took a deep breath.

'Thank you, Liam, I'd like that very much.'

Suddenly, the short blue dress she had chosen to wear today from her hastily-packed belongings felt the height of fashion. Her white sandals felt good too, worth the effort of staggering along the lane in them. She felt at her most confident, and all because of this invitation Liam had offered. Her work was pressing, and she couldn't really spare a whole morning out; but time enough to worry about that later. She might well gain inspiration from this place Liam wanted her to see, and she would work into the night if need be. She felt empowered to do anything she chose, and it was a good feeling.

There was silence between them for a moment, while around them the sounds of a successful garden party rose and fell.

He cleared his throat. 'I could collect you around nine o'clock to give us plenty of time. We'll head for The Green Beech Gallery, just off the centre of Moretonhampstead. They serve a good coffee there too. There are two or three exhibition rooms full of flower paintings in all sorts of mediums. How does that sound?'

'Incredible!'

He grinned.

'And, what's more, the owner is always on the lookout to promote more local artists. Why not take along some of your work for her to have a look at?'

'Well, yes, but — '

'You haven't any?'

She thought of the delicate botanical paintings she was preparing for the publisher. While suitable as illustrations for the book on wildflowers of the hedgerow, she couldn't quite envisage them hanging on the walls in a public exhibition. But she had nothing to lose, and it was a kind suggestion.

'One or two, perhaps.'

'I think you'll like it there.'

She had a sudden vision of his white soft-top car, and herself seated beside him, speeding through the lanes with her eyes closed and the wind in her hair. Wonderful. She smiled her acceptance of the plan; and he stepped closer, cupped her face in his hand for a magic second, and softly touched her forehead with his own.

And then he walked away and it could all have been a dream. No one had seen, she was sure of it, and no one knew that she was filled with such tenderness and longing that she wanted to hug the secret to herself for the rest of the day.

She joined Rose and Jonah, as it was time to go. She glanced sideways at Rose as they walked back across the grass to collect the pushchair, and wondered that her own delight wasn't apparent in an aura of happiness surrounding her. But Rose was chatting to Jonah, reminding him of the cakes he'd eaten and the games they had played among the bushes when he had hidden away thinking she couldn't find him. He giggled as she strapped him in, remembering too.

'It was a lovely party,' Rose said, sighing a little.

'You enjoyed yourself?' Caro asked.

'Oh, yes. And Cindy does such lovely food.'

'Cakes, Mummy,' Jonah said in satisfaction.

Caro smiled at Rose, and at young Jonah who was banging his feet against the end of the pushchair. This was the first real social occasion Rose had attended since Tom died, she thought, with a rush of sympathy. It was a beginning, and a good one. She knew in her heart that Rose wouldn't have gone if she hadn't been with her, and it was a good feeling to be useful. But to have Liam's invitation to rejoice over was the wonder of the day, and as they ambled the rest of the way in silence along the lane, it seemed to her as if she were walking on air.

Rose threw anxious looks in Caro's direction. Caro had been so quiet as they set out. Was it because she was missing her own home and regretting her decision to sell? It was a dreadful sacrifice to do this for her, and she didn't deserve it. One thing she was sure of: she would take this job if it was offered to her on Tuesday, whether she hated it or not. Yes, she would do it and hope for the best.

She looked down at Jonah.

'Shall we go and see Nana and tell her all about the party, my sweet?'

Jonah looked hopeful.

'Cake?'

'I expect so. Nana always has some for you. You wouldn't mind if I took him to see Enid, would you, Caro, since we're so close? It'll make an extra visit to her this week, and she likes that.'

Caro beamed at her. 'Not a bit of it. Go and enjoy yourselves, and give her my love.'

She would be on her own, and that was great. Liam was filling her mind to such an extent that she could think of little else.

13

Moretonhampstead was a small town high up on the eastern edge of Dartmoor. That much Caro knew, but she hadn't realised how picturesque it was, or how attractive its old buildings were in the sunshine that suddenly burst forth from behind dark clouds as they entered the town.

'It's had a long and interesting history,' Liam told her, slowing down to let a family of four cross in front of them. 'There were a few fires here in the twentieth century. They did a bit of damage, of course, but there are many Saxon and Medieval buildings left, as you can see.'

'It looks as if there's lots going on here too.'

'Oh, there is.' Liam's voice held a tinge of pride. 'And one of those things concerns the place I want you to see.'

He drove into one of the town's car parks, and she was interested to see that the attendant waved him into a place near the entrance, smiling broadly as he did so.

'Travis is an old friend of mine from university,' Liam explained as they got out and he felt in his pocket for coins to insert in the ticket machine. 'This is a bit of an act, but it amuses him to pretend to be in charge here. Rehearsing for one of his parts in the local theatre, I expect, the clown. But there you go. You can't choose your friends.'

'You can't choose your relations, you mean.'

'Is that so? I haven't many, so I wouldn't know.'

'A bit of an oversight there, then.'

He grinned at her, waved at Travis, and they walked out into the busy street. The place they were heading for was The Green Beech Gallery, and as they approached, Caro's interest quickened. Flower paintings, he had said, but that could cover a wide spectrum.

However, it was excuse enough to explain her outing with Liam to Rose, who accepted it without question, her mind on her own upcoming interview later in the day.

The door was open, and as they went inside, Caro saw at once that the reception area was large enough to house a display of tapestry work and embroidery as well as many framed prints. She picked up a leaflet that looked interesting. *Studio Workspace to Rent*, she read as she stuffed it in her bag.

'There are more exhibition rooms through there,' Liam said, indicating a door to their left. He smiled at the motherly person behind the desk and then turned back to Caro.

'Coffee first, d'you think, and then a browse?'

She hesitated, and he smiled. 'A visit to the other rooms first it is, then.'

Her idea was to look round fairly quickly, check the different styles and genres, and then return to make a closer inspection of the ones that she found most interesting. There was some lovely original work here, and she stood for a moment in front of an exuberant oil painting of poppies in a field of golden wheat. Next to it was another by the same artist, this one of bluebells spilling down a hillside. She could have gazed for hours at these and others in each of the rooms that filled her with a sense of joy so overpowering she wondered she didn't fall over. Quite unlike her own work, of course. No way could she had splashed colour onto canvas in such a liberating manner. Her gift was the delicate intricate work that she found so rewarding. She moved on to admire other styles in pastel and watercolour, but found none resembling her own.

She glanced at her watch. Time was moving too quickly. The reason for this morning's outing was for Liam to visit Mulvery Court. From what he had told her, this was a sizeable estate that had been left unattended for many years. A landscape gardener's dream. She had no idea how long this would take, but it would be unfair of her to linger here for too long.

'So, where is this coffee?' she said, returning to the reception area where Liam was chatting to the steward at the desk.

'Seen enough?' he said in surprise.

She smiled.

'I'm so glad you brought me here, Liam. It's a wonderful exhibition, and it's given me a lot to think about and take in.'

The steward looked pleased. 'But not all at once?' she said sympathetically.

Liam smiled. 'And your own work, Caro?'

She'd hoped he had forgotten. He was standing there looking expectant, and the steward seemed interested too.

'My portfolio's in the car. I brought a couple of paintings, but I don't think — '

'I'll fetch them.'

Before she could remonstrate, he had gone.

The café was a charming room at the back of the property, with a wide view of rolling countryside. Caro thought she could see Brentor in the misty distance, but her imagination might be working overtime in her anxiety about the owner being summoned to examine work she might well scorn. *But nothing ventured, nothing gained. Snap out of it, Caro.*

She smiled as they seated themselves and Liam picked up the menu.

'Hungry?'

'Not really.'

'Not even for any of those luscious apricot Danish pastries? I go for those every time. Delicious pastry oozing with flavour.'

She laughed up at him as he got up to place their order.

'You've discovered a weak spot! My mouth's watering already.'

'Danish pastries, then. And coffee . . . cappuccino, latte, filter?'

'Filter, please.'

He was back quickly, and soon afterwards a waitress appeared with a laden tray. There was a buzz of conversation now as more people came in, remarking on the charming look of the new light-wood tables and pretty flowered curtains at the window. There was the subtle scent from the white narcissi arranged in a glass bowl nearby, too.

Liam waited for a few moments, and then poured coffee for them both into the delicate china mugs.

'Flower-decorated, of course,' Caro murmured as she accepted hers. She was pleased to see four apricot pastries. One each would definitely not have been enough, she thought, as she bit into her first one.

She was still feeling dreamy from the beauty of the artwork she had seen, and she listened to Liam telling her about how the gallery had come into existence as if he were speaking from some distance away.

They got up to go, and as they left, a pleasant-faced woman, elegant in heels and trouser-suit, met them in the foyer. She smiled at Caro and held her portfolio towards her.

Caro took it. 'Oh?'

'Charming work. Thank you for letting me see something of what you can do. I'd certainly be interested in seeing more.'

'You like it?'

'Very much so.'

'It's so different from what you exhibit here.'

'Indeed. We strive for variety, and do very well. Here, let me give you my card, and I'll look forward to hearing from you. Olivia Venning.'

'Caro Anderson. Thank you.'

The white card with its gold lettering had a tiny black logo in one corner, and as they left the building, Caro saw a painting of the same image on the sign she hadn't noticed on the way in. This featured a bird hovering above a rocky outcrop that could only be Dartmoor.

'That's strange, having a bird as a logo and not a tree,' she said as they walked towards the car park.

'Not a bit of it. A sparrowhawk is of great significance to the town, if you did but know. One sparrowhawk was the annual rent set by King John in the thirteenth century. A perfect symbol for present-day Moretonhampstead, don't you think?'

She pretended to consider.

'Mmm. It depends. What if there was a shortage of sparrowhawks one year, and they couldn't produce one? That could be a problem. Was it his own idea, the king's? He might have picked something difficult deliberately.'

'But why would he do that?'

'Some people like to be difficult.' She sobered suddenly. 'I was thinking of Jared Butler. He would have chosen an albatross or a phoenix, whatever that was.'

Liam's chuckle at the foolishness of the conversation was infectious, and she laughed too. She liked that about him, the way he fell in with the talk of the moment as if it was of great importance. She still felt light-headed at Olivia Venning's appreciation of her work.

'I must say, poor Jared seems to rub people up the wrong way,' Liam said. 'Unintentionally, perhaps, like someone else I know. People find her attractive, but the words that come out of her mouth sometimes give offence, and she has no idea why. Ah well, it takes all sorts.'

They reached the main road, and he put out a hand to prevent her walking in front of a cyclist. When the man had passed, he said, 'There are plenty of sparrowhawks about today, and I expect there were in King John's time too. You can see them anywhere, and hear the noise the small birds make when they spot them hovering above them. With good reason, of course.'

'Because they catch and kill them?'

'Sparrowhawks are only small birds of prey, but males can catch birds up to thrush size, you know, and the females even bigger.'

'Wow! I didn't know that.'

They reached his car, and she waited for a moment while he clicked the switch to put the roof down. He leaned across and opened the passenger door for her.

'Okay with it down? A few miles, that's all.'

'Fine.'

They set off slowly. As they reached the edge of town, Liam put his foot down and they gained speed. Caro thought of the place they were to visit next with a stir of anticipation. It would be good to see how Liam set about his work. She had seen the briefcase he had placed in the boot of the car, and also the computer case alongside it. She supposed that he and the owner would discuss plans and ideas that she would find fascinating, and then Liam would take measurements and make notes. The visit would probably involve a lot of walking. She glanced down at her sensible shoes.

'You're okay, Caro?'

'Very much so,' she said, smiling.

Mulvery Court wasn't the huge mansion she had imagined. Built of red brick, it gave the impression that someone had knocked it up in a hurry. For a long moment, Liam stood and looked it through half-closed eyes.

'A challenge here, I think.'

He didn't sound a bit disheartened, and Caro wondered what was going on in that dark head of his. Places didn't have to be old to be beautiful, but sometimes it helped. This building had odd turrets on the corners, and a line of plain chimneypots on one end of the roof that gave it a lopsided appearance. The paint on the front door was peeling, and beside it, a zinc tub of tired-looking pansies was leaning half-off a slab of concrete that looked as if it could do with a good clean.

Liam pulled the bell-rope. They heard it jangling inside the house, but nothing happened. After a while, he pulled it again. This time, the door creaked open to reveal an elderly man in a dark suit and leaning on a walking stick, who looked anything but friendly.

'Mr Montgomery?'

'Who's asking?' The tone was suspicious.

Liam extracted a card from his wallet and held it out to him.

'I have an appointment to see you here today, Mr Montgomery, for a preliminary visit. Liam Tait, landscape garden consultant.'

'Garden consultant? What's wrong with my garden, I'd like to know?'

'There doesn't have to be anything wrong with it,' Liam said in measured tones. 'This is just a visit to see the lie of the land and agree on what needs to be done.'

'I want none of that.'

'Is there someone else here I could see, then?'

He waved his stick at them. 'Go away!'

There was no answer to that, and they had hardly turned away before the door shut behind them with a resounding crash.

Liam shrugged. 'You win some, you lose some.'

'You didn't exactly lose it because you hadn't started on it,' Caro said. 'Apart from the wasting of time, of course.'

He raised his eyebrows. 'You call it that?'

'Not on my part,' she said smartly.

He smiled.

'It's early yet, so we can take our time in getting home. We'll detour a bit, shall we, and see more of Dartmoor?'

As he edged the car out of the awkward drive, she said, suddenly anxious, 'But what are you going to do about that dreadful man?'

'I'll have to make a phone call to help clear matters up, and for that I need information that's in my office at the Manor. Afterwards, I'll run you home.'

'But — '

He glanced at her swiftly.

'You don't like the idea?'

She hesitated, a disturbing vision of the hunted expression on Jared Butler's face before her. She had tried to hide the truth from Liam in the Manor grounds because she was ashamed of scoring such an easy victory over someone she disliked and hurting him deliberately. She had always thought that truth was important in any relationship . . . until it suited her to hide it.

'I said something that wounded your agent, something I should have kept to myself. And now I'm sorry and embarrassed.'

Liam slowed down and stopped.

'Under provocation?'

'Well, yes. Sort of.'

'When was this?'

'At the tenants' party. After, as we walked across the grass, I was still shaken by the encounter with Jared, and you must have picked up on something. But I hid it from you, wanting to give the impression that everything was all right with me when it wasn't.' She looked down at her hands clenched together in her lap. 'And now I don't like the idea of seeing him again, because it brings it all back.'

'He was already employed here when I came. I expect you know that. I try to give him the benefit of the doubt for Mrs Tait's sake. So, what was it all about?'

She felt herself flush.

'He accused me of being a tenant because I was at the party.'

'And?'

'I said I was an invited guest, but he obviously wasn't.'

'Reasonable, I would have thought, in the circumstances.'

'The laughing and jeering from your other guests in the room nearly brought the house down. I should have thought before I spoke. He was devastated.'

'The man's his own worst enemy. He seems to specialise in stirring people up. He had a rotten start in life, so I've been told: bullied at school and unloved by his alcoholic mother. I led a privileged life in contrast, although I didn't realise it at the time. And not a blameless one, either. Any wrongdoing at my school had me joining in too.'

She looked at him, startled. 'You?'

'I'm flattered by your surprise.'

His eyes looked bright as he reached for her clenched hands and squeezed them. 'I expect we all have something we want to hide in our lives, something we're ashamed of, large or small. We're human, after all. The thing is to be open about it and not to fear looking vulnerable. There's a sort of freedom in that, don't you think?'

She nodded. He was right.

'So, what's it to be, then — Hovercombe Manor or Hover Cottage?'

'The Manor,' she said, convinced now there was nothing to fear. 'But I shall walk back from there.'

It certainly sounded as if Liam hadn't minded his rejection at Mulvery Court one way or the other, she thought, with a rush of sympathy.

'You're very quiet,' he said, after they had been travelling a mile or two.

'I can't help thinking of Mulvery Court and the verbal attack you got. How could anyone do such a thing?'

'I might still be in with a chance. I know he wants to be shot of the place. There's someone close to the man who believes I'm owed a huge favour, and will put in a good word for me. Time will tell.' He smiled. 'And now let's enjoy the drive home.'

'I'm certainly doing that,' she said, smiling too.

She loved the wild beauty of the landscape and the outcrops of rock on the higher ground. She saw some ponies in the distance, grazing by a stone wall, and watched them until she they were out of sight.

They arrived at Hovercombe all too soon. As Liam turned into the Manor drive, a taxi came up towards them and turned left for the village.

Liam frowned.

'Strange.'

Stranger still was the opening of the front door as they drew up alongside it. A young woman stood on the threshold, smiling at Liam as he sprang out.

14

Rose, holding Jonah by the hand, hesitated at the door into the walled garden. She had left the pushchair near the shrubs at the side of the house, hoping no one would notice it there. Jonah hadn't wanted to get out, and had wriggled as she unstrapped him, but now looked with interest at a wooden wheelbarrow containing a rake and a sieve.

'Muddy,' he said.

'Not really, young man,' said a voice behind them, making Rose jump. 'I hope you're not criticising our working methods. One of our first rules: never leave garden implements uncleaned.'

Rose smiled uncertainly at the man she presumed was going to interview her this morning. His answering smile was warm. She liked his craggy face, and the lines round his eyes that made it seem that he was going to break out in a laugh at any moment. He rubbed his hands down the sides of his corduroy trousers, and shook her hand with a firm grip.

'Kevin Masters. And you are Rose Sinclair, of course. Glad to meet you, Rose. And?'

'Jonah,' she said proudly.

'Ah, yes. Jonah. Cindy told me about him. A new recruit?'

Rose, flushing a little, looked down at her son with shining eyes and then back at Kevin. 'He's only two.'

She had wondered exactly what she would have to do for this job she had applied for so impulsively, and when Kevin took her round the vegetable garden and showed her the different beds, it all sounded strange to her. Tom had always grown potatoes and tomatoes and runner beans, ordinary vegetables, in their plot at the side of the cottage, but she had done nothing with it since his death. She must have looked a little vague as they progressed round the garden, because Kevin stopped a few times to explain things in more detail.

'You'll soon learn,' he said with confidence. He gave her a broad grin when he had shown her everything.

'You'll do, Rose. Say, next week to start? How does Monday sound? We're expecting a delivery of potting compost then, as well as bark and sand.'

Rose nodded, slightly disconcerted. Sand? She had a lot to learn.

'That's fine,' she said.

'And the young lad? I hear you've got someone staying and she'll look after him. Three days to start with, and see how we go. Does that sound good?'

'Oh yes, very good.'

'Now, let's go and drink that coffee I hope Cindy's got ready for us.'

They walked at Jonah's pace to the back door, listening to his chatter. What else had Cindy told Kevin about her? Rose wondered.

'About time too,' Cindy greeted them. She was flushed from lifting out a tray of scones from the oven, and as she straightened, Rose caught her expression of pleasure as she looked at Kevin. 'Keeping Rose talking out there for hours.'

'Exaggerating again,' Kevin said good-naturedly as he reached for one of the scones, and then dropped it hurriedly when she slapped his hand away. He laughed. 'All in good time, with luck, but I can't stay long. There are things to do.' He winked at Rose as he pulled a chair out from the table.

Cindy snorted. 'Your luck will run out if you don't behave yourself. Sit yourself down, then, and Rose too. Look what I've got for Jonah.'

The little boy gave a squeak of pleasure at the gingerbread man she gave him.

'Dumbo cakes,' he said. Rose smiled at his name for them.

There was a plate of shortbread for the others, as well as the scones warm from the oven. Cindy placed a pot of honey near the butter dish and pushed both towards Rose.

'You've been busy baking,' Rose said as she bit into the delicious softness of her scone.

'Someone has to do it with the company that's arrived. Unexpected, I can tell you.' She frowned at the butter dish. 'Standing there in her fine clothes when I opened the door, and none too pleased to find Liam missing. Elissa, she said her name was. What sort of name's that?'

'A pretty one,' Kevin observed.

Cindy rounded on him. 'Get off back to your garden.'

Kevin got up leisurely, and reached for a scone which he crammed in his mouth as he made his escape.

'You didn't give him any coffee,' Rose said.

Cindy snorted again. 'He didn't deserve it, that one.'

'He seems nice,' Rose ventured.

Cindy grabbed the coffee pot and poured Rose a generous measure. 'Get that down you,' she said, pushing the mug across to her. Then she poured orange juice for Jonah. The little boy drank, looking at her over the top of his glass with his soulful dark eyes.

'He's so like his dad,' Cindy said in softer tones.

Rose, pleased, agreed. Since the new owner had come, there weren't many workers at the Manor now who had known Tom.

But Cindy returned to the subject uppermost on her mind. 'Six suitcases she brought with her, and expected me to carry them in for her.'

'And did you?'

'More fool me.'

Cindy raised her mug to her lips, and Rose drank her coffee too, feeling a contented glow because she had got the job.

Cindy was making impatient little movements now.

'We must go,' Rose said, wiping Jonah's mouth with a tissue. 'We mustn't hold you up, Cindy. You'll have extra work now with this new guest.'

'More's the pity,' Cindy said darkly. 'She's come to stay, that one; but for how long, I'd like to know?'

As she extricated the pushchair from its hiding place and strapped Jonah in, Rose noticed that Liam's car was parked near the front door. This Elissa person would be pleased to see him, she thought, whoever she was.

*   *   *

Dark hair, curling to the shoulders of the elegant cream suit, and spindly heels. That was Caro's first impression of the newcomer as Liam leapt up the steps to the open front door and ushered her inside.

So . . . that was that. Caro got out of the car slowly and clicked shut the door. With a last glance at the vehicle that looked as abandoned as she felt herself, she started to walk up the drive to the main gate. How swiftly things changed. One minute, sheer happiness as they swept down here in his car; the next, deflation more acute than she had ever felt before. She had heard it said that one must always expect the unexpected, and this was certainly that. Liam had not even waved goodbye to her, but had headed straight for this person standing so unexpectedly in the doorway as if she had a perfect right to be there. As perhaps she had. She had noted the intimacy of her gesture as she touched Liam lightly on the arm, and had felt for a moment as if the breath had gone from her body.

The house phone rang as she unlocked the cottage door. The large porch felt cold, and the passage beyond seemed dimmer than usual.

She reached for the phone. 'Hello? Hover Cottage.'

'Caro, what must you think of me?'

Her heart thudded at the sound of his voice. She hadn't allowed herself to think anything on the walk home other than that she didn't belong here. Liam's private life had nothing to do with her.

He had invited her to accompany him on his visit to Mulvery Court because there was the opportunity to call at The Green Beech Gallery, which he knew would be of interest to her. Liam was a kind man who thought of the welfare of others. That was all. She had no right to read more into it.

She cleared her throat.

'I had already offered to walk home,' she pointed out. 'No need to worry about getting me back, Liam.' Her tone was relaxed, as if she didn't mind one way or the other. Walking on her own or being driven back was all the same to her, whether or not Liam was at her side. She drew herself up to her full height, proud of herself.

Strangely, he seemed to find it difficult to reply, and she had time to wonder again exactly who this woman was who seemed to affect him so deeply.

'Thank you for taking me with you today,' she added in a formal tone of voice she hardly recognised as her own.

Come, she could do better than that. 'I enjoyed, it, Liam.' That was more friendly, and she wasn't going to sound needy. 'And the rest doesn't matter.'

'I was surprised to see Elissa, you see. I thought she was abroad, and then to see her there was a shock. Things are going to work out as I hoped because of her. But I should have introduced you. I'm sorry, Caro. I'll be in touch again very soon, I promise. The day was good for me too. I appreciate your under-standing, Caro, and I'll see you soon.'

He clicked off and she stared down at the receiver in her hand. Then, very carefully, she replaced the phone in its cradle and went into the living room. Fluffy got up from his place on the sofa and stretched. His purr deepened as she picked him up and buried her face in his long, soft fur. She felt the rumbling deep inside him and was comforted. Liam had said he'd enjoyed the day. She had, too, until they arrived back at the Manor. She wouldn't think of it any more.

She had one obvious thing to do now, and that was to concentrate on her work and complete it to her satisfaction before the weekend. She had allowed herself to believe that Liam felt the same way about her as she did for him, but that didn't mean it was true. A brief kiss on the forehead on a mild spring day did not mean anything other than friendship. And neither did the warmth of his smile, or his interest in her love of painting that had resulted in the visit to the gallery. And now she was left with the feeling of emptiness and of being alone. She must do everything she could to fill that vacuum and not give the slightest hint of it to anyone. She had work to do and deliver before she was free to look after Jonah, and that must be her first consideration.

Fluffy seemed pleased when she put him down on the sofa again. He curled up at once into a comfortable purring ball. If only she could do the same and blot out the memory of Liam's kind face and smile, and of the way he seemed so protective of her happiness that she had assumed was for herself alone.

But onwards and upwards! She had things to do.

She was hard at work on a delicate white stitchwort when she heard the sound of Rose and Jonah's return. For a moment she stayed where she was, taking deep calming breaths before she got up to greet them, prepared to hear about Rose's visit to a place that hurt her now even to think about.

'And there's something else, Caro,' Rose said when she got to the end of her tale and had enquired about Caro's morning. 'Someone called Elissa has come to stay at the Manor. Cindy's afraid she's come for good.'

Caro clenched her hands so that her knuckles showed white.

'Oh? D'you know who she is?'

Rose shook her head. 'I don't think Cindy knows either. I didn't see her myself. Maybe I will when I start work next week.'

Rose's heightened colour as she talked of her new job gave a her a look of confidence that had been sadly lacking lately.

'I need to work extra-hard for the next few days,' Caro said. 'I plan to travel up to London by car via Bridport this time and deliver to the publisher on Friday, if that's all right with you.'

Rose smiled. 'Of course it is, Caro.'

'I'll stay the night in Bridport on the way, and on the way back too. I need to do a bit of sorting-out and perhaps see the solicitor.'

'To tell him the sale of your house is off now I'll be earning some money?'

'Well, no.' Caro paused. Rose was so happy at the moment about helping herself financially, and she hated to crush that happy look. 'I couldn't do that to Sandy, and I wouldn't want to anyway. We must see how this job goes. I'm pleased for you, Rose, I really am, but I don't want you to be under any pressure.'

'It'll be lovely having you close by for keeps,' Rose said. She sounded a little doubtful, but then she stepped forward and gave Caro a huge hug. 'Let's do something nice to celebrate,' she said, her voice muffled.

'If you're sure you really want me nearby?'

Rose gave a shaky laugh. 'It'll be the best thing in the world for me. How about I open that special wine I've been saving? How does that sound, Caro?'

15

The sense of achievement that Caro expected to wash over her on the completion of her painting commission didn't happen. At any other time, praise from the publisher would have filled her with relief at a job well done. Even now, seated in the train that was due to pull out of Waterloo station at any moment, she felt only a strange emptiness. Everything had gone well, especially the drive to Bridport yesterday and Sandy's warm welcome. The early start from Bridport this morning meant little traffic. She had made sure that her portfolio was safely in the boot of her car as she drove to Dorchester South railway station. The London train had been on time and fairly empty, and the sun shining.

Her usual sense of exciting urgency when visiting the capital had been sadly lacking today as she had struggled to banish thoughts of Liam. A vision of his face intruded at unexpected moments and stirred her peace of mind. She missed his laid-back charm, and the way he listened to everything she said with his head held a little to one side in concentration.

Now, as the train slid out of the station, Caro leaned back in her seat and closed her eyes, willing herself to dwell on other, more important things, like house-hunting in or around Hovercombe. She thought of Rose's face glowing with pleasure at her job offer, to be followed soon after by apprehension. With Caro living nearby, the pressure would be off; and if the job was too worrying for Rose, she could leave.

Caro opened her eyes and sat up. She must do something about it at once. She pulled out her smartphone to start some research online. Why not Moretonhampstead? No, it had taken them quite a while to drive there the other day. The weather had been kind then, but in deep winter it would be a different story.

They were whipping past Wimbledon now. She stared out of the window at the factories, the houses, the streaking stations. Okehampton, to the north of the moor, was Rose's nearest town. Common sense told her that this would be a good place to start. She clicked on Okehampton Estate Agents and then checked on one of the websites. The number of houses on offer looked promising, and she selected one within her price range, checking first the photos and then the details. Then she looked at the others that seemed at first glance to be suitable too.

She heard the clatter of an approaching trolley.

'Tea, madam, coffee?'

'Not for me, thanks.'

'Something to eat?'

'No, really. I'm okay.'

By the time they reached Winchester,

she had discarded three more properties. This narrowed it down a little. She looked again at the others, more critically this time. One of them, on the outskirts of town, had a large, unkempt garden offering a greenhouse and an outbuilding that could be made into a suitable workroom for her painting; but the kitchen was tiny and there was only one bedroom. Another had three bedrooms but was situated in a place called Upperdung. This was slightly off-putting, and for all she knew might be miles away on the other side of town.

She gazed out of the window once more at the flying countryside. Surely there was something among this lot that was suitable? Another estate agent? Well, why not? She hadn't finished yet.

This time, one in particular stood out from the rest. This was in the vicinity of a place that sounded familiar, somewhere near Bridestowe where Liam had had to brake suddenly to avoid a black cat that had taken it into its head to dive straight across the road in front of them. She had admired his swift reaction, and the calm way he'd gathered speed again as they left the village behind them.

She took a deep breath and then clicked on the details of the property. Small kitchen and lounge-cum-dining room, two bedrooms, bathroom. Large garden with shed. No garage or parking space. Good views from rear of property. Then the photos. The patio doors overlooking fields and hills looked great. Yes, she could live with that. She smiled, imagining an early morning at this time of the year with the mist unfurling from those Dartmoor hills, sunshine sparkling on the dewy grass and the twitter of sparrows enjoying the seeds sprinkled for them on the mossy patio. The living quarters were a little cramped, with no space downstairs to work comfortably, but in time perhaps the shed could be fitted out with electricity if it wasn't too big a job, so she could work out there.

And she would be only a a few miles away from Hovercombe. Definitely a bonus.

She clicked on the others again. Most of them had no land attached, with no opportunity to fit out an exterior building to serve as her studio. No good to her, sadly.

She gazed at her phone, deep in thought. Then she dialled the phone number of the estate agent to enquire about the only property that felt right.

★ ★ ★

She knew that no property was going to be one hundred percent perfect; however, it was one thing to understand that in theory, but quite another to be disappointed on viewing a place that had seemed promising until she saw it for herself. She had made an appointment to meet the estate agent there at eleven o'clock on Monday morning, because that would give her plenty of time to clear and wash up the breakfast things, and for Jonah to settle down with her in charge instead of his mother. When it was time to go, he was pleased to be buckled into his car seat, and they set off in good time. It seemed a nice idea to drive around a bit and explore the immediate area.

'Cows,' piped up Jonah, from the back of the car.

'Plenty of cows,' Caro agreed. 'Ponies too, I expect, if we knew where to look.'

'Look?' said Jonah, interested.

She was beginning to feel excited now, and Jonah must have picked up on it because he began to giggle and bang his toy lamb on the back of her seat.

'Steady now, Jonah, she said. 'Caro's going to park the car now, and we're going to get out and look at a house. Then, if you're a good boy, we'll go and look for ponies afterwards.'

He seemed satisfied with that, and was happy enough trotting at her side as they made their way to the gate where the estate agent was waiting for them.

'Man,' Jonah said, sounding friendly.

He looked familiar. Surely . . . ? Caro stopped and stared.

'We've met before,' he said, coming forward to shake her hand. 'I'm Arnold Beesley. It's Caro, isn't it? Miss Caro Anderson, since we're on formal business. Rose introduced us, if you remember.'

She remembered well enough, but meeting him here was a surprise. She had thought him stocky when they met briefly on her arrival at Hover Cottage. Now he seemed to have gained a few more pounds. He gripped her hand a little too firmly, as if emphasising the importance of this appointment.

She stepped back a little. 'Tom's cousin, or second cousin, I think you said.' She smiled a little tentatively. 'But what are you doing here?'

He held up his clipboard.

'I was lucky to get a position locally.' He looked knowingly at her as if she fully understood the implications. 'Payne and Gilbert are a good firm to work for, and I need to be on

180

the spot. An estate agent, what could be better?'

Better for what? She murmured a noncommittal reply and hoped she didn't look too bemused. Rose couldn't have known about this, or she would have told her.

He moved his weight from one foot to the other. 'I have the details of the property here for you. Shall we go inside?'

'Yes, of course.'

'It's been on the market for some time, I understand, and they've reduced the price. It just needs the right person to come along.' His smile seemed to indicate that she was definitely that.

The front garden was overgrown to such an extent that it was hard to pick out the path, but the door, a bright red, had obviously been recently painted because she caught a faint smell of turpentine as they got close. She stood aside for it to be unlocked, still wondering how it had come about that this man was living and working locally with Rose having no idea of it.

The narrow hall smelt damp, and there were dark patches on the cream walls. The kitchen at the far end was so tiny that there was hardly room for the three of them to squeeze in. No, this wasn't for her.

'I don't think — ' she began.

Arnold Beesley consulted his clipboard as if for inspiration.

'Upstairs?' he said brightly. 'Lead the way, young man.'

Caro urged Jonah forward, wanting to get this over with as soon as possible. But Arnold, it appeared, was in no hurry. He lingered on the landing after her brief inspection of the two bedrooms so that she found it impossible to get past.

'Such a good area,' he said. 'And this is a bargain at the price. Rose should do very well here.'

'Rose?'

'I take it you are here on her behalf.'

It was a statement and not a question. He gave her no time to reply even if she hadn't been stunned by his words.

'A good decision, if I may say so, Miss Anderson, and I need to be around. The cottage will be perfect for my needs. My old mate wants me nearby so we can get going on our plans.'

'Plans?'

The shifty look she had glimpsed at their first meeting flitted across his face. He tapped his nose.

'I've said too much. Hush-hush. I'll say no more.'

He was standing a little too close, and she felt uncomfortable.

'I think I've seen enough now, Mr Beesley. I'll be in touch.'

He moved aside and then followed them downstairs.

'Hush-hush,' he said again as they emerged into daylight. 'I'm sure you understand. Plenty of potential with this place, tell her. I'm at the other end of the phone when she wants to make an appointment to view the place for herself. It'll be good to see her again.'

'It's not for Rose, Mr Beesley.'

'Some things are best kept under wraps. Am I right?'

'Technically, perhaps, but not in this case — '

'Enough said,' he agreed.

She bid him farewell and hurried Jonah down the uneven path. There was much to think about here. Arnold wanted to be on the spot — but which spot? The Hovercombe Manor Estate? She had the distinct impression that it was so, or why keep his presence in the area secret from Rose but hint that he wanted her cottage? And who was this friend of his who wanted him close?

She had no heart for further property visiting now, and in any case Jonah needed a sleep. He was already nodding his head forward as she buckled him into his car seat, all thoughts of ponies forgotten. She set off slowly, deep in thought. Seeing Tom's cousin was odd, and even now she wondered if she had dreamed the past half-hour. If only she had! She dared not think what Rose would make of it. She certainly wouldn't be happy knowing that Arnold had designs on Hover Cottage.

16

'I'll never get them clean again,' Rose said, looking down at her fingernails.

Caro couldn't help smiling at her doleful expression. Rose was exaggerating, of course, and being parted from Jonah had much to do with it. Each time she returned from the Manor she seemed more downcast than the time before, and yet she had only been working there for a short while. She had always been proud of her hands, and planting out seedlings was dirty work. Gardening gloves? No way. They only impeded the delicate tasks she had been set.

Caro smiled again. 'You're doing a good job, and I'm proud of you.'

'But it means you're not getting on with your own work. Oh Caro, it's not good, is it?'

Looking after Jonah was more strenuous than Caro had expected. He was missing his mother, and was hard to settle for his daily rest. The only thing to do was to take him out for long periods, and hope the movement of car or pushchair would lull him to sleep. Her house-hunting wasn't going well, and that was worrying. Even when Rose was home, the confines of Hover Cottage meant it was hard to concentrate on her painting when household sounds and the demands of a two-year-old were all around her. She needed her own place for that.

'Peace of mind is what we both need, Rose. And you're doing your best to make sure we get it. When Bully Butler next strikes, you'll be ready for him, waving great wads of extra cash.'

Rose smiled too, and cheered up a little. But Caro still felt drained at her efforts not to think of Liam, whatever she was doing. A few weeks ago, they hadn't even met; and now here he was, filling her mind at every turn. Rose had told her that Elissa was still in residence, but that Liam had been called away almost as soon as she had turned up, and no one had any further news of him. Cindy was threatening to hand in her notice, and Kevin was upset at the thought of not seeing Cindy again even though she never appeared to have a good word for him.

But that was none of her business. Liam had promised to be in touch. She must be content with that.

'I didn't tell you, Rose,' she said. 'I met Tom's cousin the other day.'

'Arnold?'

The expression on Rose's face would have made Caro smile at any other time, but this was serious because of the connection with the estate.

'But where?'

'Remember that cottage I looked at near Bridestowe? He was the estate agent who showed me round. He's working for Payne and Gilbert in Okehampton. It's just a bit worrying, you see. I needed to think about it before I mentioned it.'

Rose still looked dumbfounded. 'But why?'

'I'll make us a coffee and I'll tell you what I think.'

Bemused, Rose put down the duster in her hand, and then picked it up again and twisted it into a knot.

'He seemed all right the day he came, didn't he? I remember Tom saying . . . ' Rose broke off and looked dreamily into space.

'What, Rose? What did he say?'

'When they were boys, Arnold wanted Tom to do something not quite right. He wouldn't do it, though. Arnold went into such a dreadful rage that Tom was scared.'

Caro smiled. 'He looked so stolid when he was here, didn't he? He was like that yesterday. A bit impatient, but that was all.'

She poured boiling water onto the instant coffee in two mugs. For the first time she wondered if Liam was aware that one of his employees was planning to go into business with this

Arnold Beesley, which seemed to rest on his occupancy of Hover Cottage. The agent would deal with arranging that, of course, if Rose handed in her notice. But that wasn't going to happen. Not while she was here to fight Rose's battles. Since the sale of her own place hadn't yet been finalised, Rose's earning of extra money was important.

'Tom's cousin!' Rose said. 'I trusted him. Tom would have too. I know he would.'

She was near to tears, and only Jonah's waking cries had her springing up and dashing off to see to him. When she came back, she was holding the little boy tightly to her, and resisting his struggles to be put down.

'I'll work harder than ever. I'll get to like it, just see if I don't. This is Tom's home too, and Jonah's. He's not taking it away from us.'

'Fighting talk. Go for it, girl!'

Caro watched Jonah shake himself free of his mother and then give her a toothy grin before heading for his toy-box.

It was only too clear that with Liam away from home, Jared Butler would choose this time to set any plans of his own in motion. Caro daily expected another missive declaring his intentions to increase the rent if she didn't return home and leave Rose to her own devices. Goodness knew what he would get up to if she wasn't here. She didn't trust him one little bit.

Liam's promised communication came early the next day. Caro's latest commission was one that differed from the others insofar as it involved wide landscapes in ink instead of her delicate close-ups of various plants and flowers. Today, she had risen earlier than usual. She made herself a mug of tea and then set to work at the rickety table in her small bedroom.

Her mobile signalled the arrival of a text. She stared at the words on the screen — Liam's words — and took a deep breath.

I know my swift exit from Hovercombe means I owe you an apology and an explanation, Caro, but it must wait till my return. Elissa and I go back a long way and I'm concerned about her. Would you contact her to check she's OK? Thanks.

She read it again. She placed her phone on the table before her, and looked at it as if it was to blame for this sore hurt she was feeling. There could be no more work for her now until she had done what he asked. She put out a finger to reply immediately, but then thought better of it. This needed thinking about. She would do it, of course, but she needed to work out exactly when.

She screwed the lid back on her liquid paint and stood up.

★ ★ ★

Caro lifted Jonah out of his pushchair and rang the bell on the front door of the manor house. On the way here, she had debated with herself the best way to go about this, and had dismissed the idea of encountering Cindy first by using the back entrance.

'Door shut,' Jonah said. 'Mummy?'

Caro smiled down at him, holding his hand tightly.

'Not yet, Jonah. Pretty lady first.'

Her anxiety was increasing by the minute. She pressed the bell, and after a long silence pressed it again. She bit her lip, considering. Two options — try the back door, or go home again. The first, of course, however much she disliked the idea. She strapped Jonah back into the pushchair and set off on the long way around the house so that they passed the orangery where Liam had held his house-warming lunch for the tenants. Today was gloomy, with lowering clouds that threatened rain. It didn't auger well, and neither did the raised voices from the open door of the orangery.

Caro stopped abruptly, the tyres of the pushchair skidding on the damp paving stones. Inside the building, Cindy was glaring at the other woman, who stood firmly with feet apart, clutching a pile of coloured tablecloths to her as if afraid that they would be snatched away at any moment.

'Give them here! They're mine.'

'Yours?' The contempt was clear in Elissa's clipped voice.

Cindy's nostrils flared. 'Mine.'

She took a step towards her, but Elissa didn't move. Jonah wriggled in his seat and let out a cry.

Caro felt a pounding in her ears as adrenaline rushed through her body. 'Stop it, both of you. You're frightening Jonah!'

Cindy took one horrified look at the child and seemed to deflate instantly, while Elissa stood back, her chest heaving. 'She's jeopardising my plans!'

'That's enough, the pair of you.' She bent to release Jonah from his pushchair and give him a reassuring hug.

'Cindy's going to look after you, Jonah,' she said, 'while Elissa and I have a talk.'

'Pretty lady?' Jonah said uncertainly, looking from one to the other.

'Pretty lady. Cindy, take him!'

A moment's silence. Elissa had visibly relaxed now, and was brushing strands of hair away from her face. Caro felt sorry for her. Someone should have warned her of Cindy's hot temper. It was easy to imagine how this row had started if Elissa tried to act the lady of the manor with someone like Cindy, who was so sure of her own importance in the running of the place.

Then Cindy rushed to Jonah and took his hand. 'Come and see what Cindy's got for you, my love.'

'Dumbo cakes?'

His eyes brightened as she mentioned the gingerbread men she made only for him, and he took no more persuading.

17

'Won't you come inside?' Elissa said when they had gone. 'Is that your little boy? A dear little chap, and surprisingly fond of the housekeeper.'

'His mother's a friend of hers. I'm his aunt, Caro Anderson.'

'Oh.' For a moment she looked confused. Then she said, confident again, 'Elissa Montgomery.'

'I'm also a friend of Liam's. He's asked me to call in and say hello.' Well, not quite like that, but it was near enough.

Elissa smiled and then shrugged. 'You've caught me at a bad moment, I'm afraid. All a question of these tablecloths I found in a kitchen drawer. Just the thing for the little tables in here in the orangery, don't you think?' She looked round for somewhere to place the cloths and, finding nowhere, indicated that Caro should follow her into the adjoining room where she put them down on the table by the window.

'While I'm here, I'm going to help Liam set up a tearoom,' she said. 'A good idea, don't you think?'

'But I understood that Cindy is to be in charge of getting that organised?'

'The housekeeper? I don't think so. It needs someone with flair and acumen, good with the public and able to show the place off to the best advantage. Let me order some coffee to be brought to us now in the sitting room.'

Caro hesitated. Not a good idea. She could just imagine Cindy's reaction to that; and there was Jonah to consider.

'Perhaps another time.'

'Then let's find ourselves a seat in here, shall we?'

Caro chose a chair near the open door and Elissa seated herself nearby. The room they were in seemed larger than when the luncheon buffet had been laid out on long tables, when it had been so crowded that Caro hasn't realised its size. Now, with them removed and easy chairs reinstalled, she could see that it must once have been one of the main reception rooms. The portraits on the walls seemed to indicate that. Family members of the last century, she presumed, looking somewhat rigid in their ornate frames. Too dark, though. They looked as if they could do with some sensitive restoring, but even then she doubted if they would be anything more than second-rate.

She glanced at Elissa, who was leaning back in her chair with one elegant leg crossed over the other.

'So, you're a friend of Liam's?' Elissa said with interest. 'Living locally? He and I go back a long way.' Her eyes softened. 'We met at university, you know. He did something for me that was so kind, and I'll never forget it. That's why I'm here now. It seems so long ago.'

She paused as if expecting a compliment about the obvious shortness of that time. But not from her, Caro thought. She knew that Liam's training as an architect had been a long one.

The pause lengthened, and Elissa shot her a sharp glance before saying, 'Liam wasn't studying accountancy like me, of course.'

'And you like it here?'

'Liam will, too, when I help get his project up and running. No need for him then to be off all over the place any more, don't you think?'

She was so sure of herself that Caro began to feel diminished. There was no longer any need for her to stay. Elissa was well and thriving, and that was what Liam wanted to hear. Too thriving, it seemed, but that was none of her business.

Elissa gave a happy sigh. 'Oh yes, I'm keeping so busy getting it all arranged.'

'Online?' Caro queried.

'How else?' Elissa's smile was condescending. 'Early stages yet, but I have connections that will make all the difference.'

Caro wanted to ask if she had invaded Liam's study to use his computer, but didn't know how to do it without sounding suspicious. She stood up and glanced at the tablecloths on the table behind her. 'I'll take these back to the kitchen, shall I?'

'If you like.'

Caro picked them up. The room felt stuffy now, and the damper, cooler air outside was a relief. The mown-grass scent was pleasant too, and so was a woodpigeon's soothing coo-coo somewhere in the distance.

Cindy took the pile of tablecloths from her gingerly. 'They'll get a wash.'

Caro smiled. 'As bad as that?'

'Worse. Come on in.'

'How has Jonah been?'

'Quiet. Too quiet, and he's not eaten anything.'

'Not even the sweets?

'Not even his favourite dumbo cakes. I'll pop them in a bag for him to take home.'

Neither mentioned the confrontation

Caro had interrupted, but Cindy was tight-lipped as they left. Caro had become used to her threats to hand in her notice at the slightest provocation, but none were forthcoming this time when perhaps she had good reason. This alone warned her of trouble ahead. Elissa had seemed confident of her authority and talked of connections. A burst of insight struck her. Could it be that Arnold was one of them? A disturbing thought, but one that needed considering.

She had intended to go straight back to Hover Cottage and text Liam from there when she had put Jonah down for his rest, but the opportunity to call in at the walled garden was there and she took it.

She saw Rose immediately She was dealing with some bags of compost, and looking as if she knew exactly what she was doing as she emptied some into containers on a trolley and patted down the soil with a confident hand. She looked up and saw them, and her face brightened.

'Mummy,' Jonah cried, and burst into tears.

Immediately Rose was down at his side, her muddied hands forgotten in her haste to unclip him from the pushchair and hug him to her.

'He feels hot.'

'He didn't eat the sweets Cindy gave him, not even those dumbo cakes.'

'He's ill.'

Caro could see that there was a flushed look about him now, and he had dropped his bag of goodies on the path. She picked it up.

Rose rocked him backwards and forwards, murmuring softly while Caro stood to one side watching them. It was hard not to feel ineffectual in the face of this mother-love, but she had to do something. She found Kevin in the shed he had set up for repotting his delicate plants. He looked harassed.

He listened to Caro's words with his head a little to one side.

'She needs to take him home and look after him herself,' he said.

'I'll tell her.'

He frowned. 'I'm heavily involved here, but we've an order of building materials arriving any minute.'

'In the garden?'

'To be kept out of sight of the house, the boss said.'

'And there's not much room?'

Kevin scratched his head as he came out and regraded the sacks of compost that were obviously in the way. She could see that something was wrong in the way he was standing. His confident stance was gone. He shuffled one foot in the dust on the path. 'I'd better get these moved.'

'Can I help?'

He could see she meant it by the way she straightened his shoulders. 'You're serious?'

'Tell me what to do.'

Rose, relieved, departed with Jonah at once, and Caro set to work. Filling the remainder of the pots on the trolley was easy, and after that she helped Kevin move it to just inside the gate where they could be placed well to one side, and the containers looked good against the old brickwork of the wall.

'Do they need planting up now?'

'I'll show you.'

This was an enjoyable job, and Caro settled down to arranging the small petunia plants in such a way that they intermingled with the alyssum and would provide a lovely show of bright colours later in the season. In her mind's eye she could see their lovely display, and smiled as she worked. Fortunately, she was wearing her flat shoes and her oldest jeans, suitable for most odd jobs around the place. She hadn't wanted to be seen as attempting to rival Elissa's elegant attire. Not that she could, of course, but there was no harm in pretending. And now her choice was paying off. She smiled as she went inside the building to wash her hands and found Kevin, forehead puckered, examining a pile of papers placed on top of one of the cabinets.

He smiled when he saw her, and rubbed one hand over his hair. 'Job done? Great.'

'And now?'

'Wanting more?'

'Why not?'

'Mug of tea first. I'll get the kettle on.'

While they were drinking from the huge white mugs that Kevin got down from the top shelf, she heard footsteps outside, and Cindy appeared carrying a familiar cake tin.

She thrust it at Kevin. 'These need eating.'

Kevin opened the tin and eyed the contents hungrily. 'Stale, are they?'

Cindy ignored his insinuation. 'Madam's on the warpath. She'll be heading this way, sticking her nose into everything. I came to warn you.' She emptied the macaroons from the tin onto an open ledger. 'Get these down you, and stop arguing.'

Caro smiled again as she took one. She stood back a little, listening to the banter between the two of them that was obviously enjoyed by both. But Cindy didn't linger for long. She gathered up her empty tin and was off.

18

The building materials arrived half an hour late, and by the time the lorry reversed inside the open gateway for unloading, Kevin had made sure that there was available space.

'This is for the extension to make the new shop and reception area,' he said proudly when the delivery lorry had gone rumbling off. 'The boss doesn't waste time.'

And neither did Jared Butler, it seemed. He came swinging into the garden ten minutes later when Caro was helping Kevin move some of the smaller items to a more convenient place. His eyes narrowed as he saw her. 'What are you doing here?'

Caro got up from a kneeling position and rubbed down the front of her jeans. A strange expression flitted across his face. Surely he couldn't be plotting revenge on Rose because of her absence this morning?

Kevin emerged from the potting shed, drying his hands on a piece of rag. 'Hi, Jared. What can we do for you?'

Jared indicated Caro with a flick of his wrist. 'You can explain her presence here, for a start.'

'She's working for me, filling in for someone else due to illness.'

'The girl's ill? She looked all right to me. I don't believe that for a minute. It's a conspiracy. I'll need to check up on her and see what she's got to say for herself. Then watch out.' He threw a look of dislike at Caro. 'The boss'll hear about this.'

The click of the garden gate made him spin round. 'Elissa?'

Her smile encompassed them all. 'Trouble?'

'Oh yes, big trouble.' Jared's smile was triumphant.

Elissa raised an eyebrow. 'Is that so? I saw you coming here, Jared, and I heard what you said. We need to talk. Now.'

He glared. 'Now? I'm not moving from here until I've got to the bottom of this.'

'I've been looking into things on Liam's behalf, and suspect there's a discrepancy in the accounts. I thought I should warn you.'

Jared laughed scornfully. 'Oh, yeah? Tell me more.'

'Luckily for you, I picked up on it in time.'

'What do you mean, 'picked up on it'? You've been in the study, at the boss's computer? How did you — ?'

'It can be done.' Elissa's calm expression didn't flicker. 'I'm considering the idea of a print-out as a back-up,' she added reflectively. 'Serious fraud, don't you think?'

'Anyone can make a slip-up,' he snarled.

'Don't tell me it wasn't deliberate.'

Jared looked from one to the other, a hunted expression on his face.

Kevin, standing well back, cleared his throat. 'So there's nothing for me to worry about at the moment?'

Elissa smiled. 'Or any of us, except Mr Butler here.'

The hint of a threat in Elissa's voice as she looked at Jared seemed designed to make the position clear. 'No more trying to bully the people here. And no more dishonesty. Do you understand, Jared Butler?'

Jared scowled, glared round at them and slunk off.

Elissa dusted off her hands, a smile touching the corners of her mouth. She waited until Kevin had returned to his work and then said, 'That went off well.'

' So what was it all about?'

'A guilty conscience on his part, don't you think? He looked so furtive coming here to spy on what you lot were doing, so it occurred to me to see what he was up to and put a stop to it.'

'You don't mean — ?'

'Well, wouldn't you if you had the opportunity? Serve him right, don't you think? I told no lies. I accused him of nothing. His conscience did the rest. And what's a little implied lie between friends?'

Caro laughed. 'Hardly friends.'

Elissa gave her a brief smile. 'Definitely not now. But who cares? I have a feeling our Jared won't be around much longer. I'll leave you to it to work in peace.'

Caro looked at her with respect. 'Thank you. The end result was good, even if your tactics were a little dubious.'

Elissa grinned. 'They worked, though, didn't they?'

Caro had a lot to think about for the rest of the morning. She was grateful to Elissa, but all the same there was a niggle deep down that wouldn't go away. When they met earlier, she hadn't entertained the possibility of Elissa having a quick-thinking mind and sense of fair play. She had misjudged her. So, what did that make Caro? Arrogant, for a start, and a bad judge of character. Not at all nice.

She walked home quickly, anxious now to be with Rose and Jonah in the comfort of Hover Cottage, asking how Jonah was and hopefully finding him much better. And she would text Liam to tell him that Elissa was getting on well, and making herself at home at the Manor. He would be grateful to her for checking, and that would be that. She would leave it to Elissa to voice her misgivings about Jared's honesty.

★ ★ ★

Work, work, work! Well, yes, that was the idea. By now she had accumulated enough to make a second visit to The Green Beech Gallery in Moretonhampstead worthwhile. Olivia Venning had invited her to get in touch when she had more to show her, even though most of it was destined for the Winter Exhibition at The Clover Gallery in London. Olivia's appreciation had been motivating, and now was the time to do something about it.

Rose wasn't working the following day, and Jonah was a different boy from that of the previous afternoon, when it had seemed as if he might be sickening for something. Bully Butler seemed unlikely to pose a threat. A quick phone call to make arrangements, and she was off.

She chose a different route this time, a longer one, because she had plenty of time and wanted to explore more of the countryside, even if it meant driving on narrow twisting lanes. By the time she had rattled over a cattle grid and onto rising ground, she felt light-hearted enough to hum a few snatches of *Widecombe Fair*. She broke off, laughing at herself. It was a glorious morning, and the air was astir through the open window with shimmering light. Even Liam's absence could make no difference to her feeling of wellbeing. She was a free woman, able to make her own decisions. But if it wasn't for Liam, a small inner voice reminded her, she wouldn't be here now driving towards what she hoped would make a huge difference to her life. Yes, that was how it was, and Liam understood that. He believed in her, that was all.

Sobering a little, she slowed down as she reached the outskirts of the town. Liam's friend greeted her in the car park as if he wasn't at all surprised to see her here again. His grin was infectious and she smiled back.

'Liam not with you this time?'

'Not this time.' She busied herself getting her portfolio out of the car, and when she looked up he was deep in conversation with another customer, looking as cheerful as ever. Glancing up, he gave her a wave.

This time, Olivia Venning was waiting to greet her in the foyer, and ushered her into a light airy room to one side of the main door. The coffee machine was purring, but there was business to be done before they could make use of it.

Caro had the impression of bare white walls and space, and little furniture apart from a large table in the centre of the room, a desk by the window, and a smaller table at the side of the door on which stood the coffee-making equipment. Without the sunshine on this side of the building it would have looked cheerless if it hadn't been for the large pot plant in the centre of the desk with its purple flowers each centred in white.

'That's Kim,' Olivia said as she saw her glance at it. 'A streptocarpus. He's rather special.' A small smile lingered at the corner of her mouth. 'But let's see what you've brought me.'

Caro had almost dreaded this moment, but there was something about Olivia that inspired confidence, and she spread out her work at once and then stood back a little. Olivia said nothing, but Caro could see that she was impressed as she inspected each painting with great care.

'I have the feeling that these are executed with love,' Olivia said.

Caro felt warmth flood her cheeks. 'You like them?'

Olivia raised one of them to take a closer examination, and Caro could see that it was the one of the small white stitchwort she had been working on when Rose had returned from the Manor with talk of the new arrival. Since then, she had come to know Elissa for herself, and found her surprisingly savvy where Jared was concerned, plus anxious to look after Liam's interests. She owed her for coming to the rescue of Rose's good name when Jared seemed intent on blackening it. But it was hard to wish her well, however much she struggled.

Olivia turned to her. 'You're frowning, my dear.

'Oh, I'm sorry.'

'You don't like this one? But it's charming. I think it's my favourite of them all.'

Caro nodded. 'I agree with you. There's something about such a dainty little thing that I found appealing.'

'Then that's why it's done with such delicacy. And you say that they all destined for the London gallery?'

'The Clover, yes.'

'And you'd like to take part in an exhibition here too?'

This was what she had hoped for, but hearing it from Olivia herself was wonderful. She smiled, and felt her whole face shining with enthusiasm. 'I would like it more than anything.'

Olivia smiled too.

'You realise, of course, that you would be required for stewarding? The success of any exhibition here depends on its contributors, and on them being on-call for emergency stewarding at a moment's notice. Would that be accept-able?'

'Oh, yes. I'd feel privileged to do it.'

She would work all the hours at her disposal, Caro thought, with this end in sight. Living somewhere in the area was obviously essential, and that wouldn't be a problem.

Olivia's office was the venue for drinking their coffee today, and Olivia carried the tray of coffee pot and cups the short distance so that over the Danish pastries already there they could discuss the business details.

When at last these were completed, Olivia stood up and clasped Caro's hands with her own.

'Here's to a successful venture,' she declared with a smile.

Caro walked back to the car park with a spring in her step.

19

Action! Enough of this waffling about house-hunting. Conditions were cramped in Hover Cottage, and for everyone's sake Caro needed her own place. Somewhere between here and Hovercombe would be perfect. Any day now, Sandy and Bob would be in a position to exchange contracts.

'You're looking happy,' Liam's friend Travis greeted her as she approached her car.

'You too.'

'Always happy, me.'

'I can believe it, living in this attractive town. Any spare houses on the market to suit me, I wonder?'

He pushed his car park-attendant's cap to the back of his head. 'Are you actively looking?'

'Pity this place is a bit far away for what I want.'

'Nearer Hovercombe Manor?'

She felt herself flush and said quickly, 'The village of Hovercombe is where I'd like to be. Or somewhere not too far away.' A second's silence, and then she added, 'For personal reasons.' *And what sort of reasons were they if not to be near Liam?* That was what he was thinking. She could see it his smile and in the twinkle in his eye.

'I see.'

He didn't, but explaining was useless.

'There's nothing suitable in Oke-hampton at the moment,' she said, 'and I'm wanting something straight away.'

'Tavistock?'

'It's an idea. I might drive back that way and see what's on offer.'

'Good luck, then.'

She got into to her car, anxious to be off. The villages between Tavistock and Hovercombe would be good, she thought, as she drove out of town. It would be a new route to her, which she knew from the map would take her across the centre of the moor.

She found it easily enough. At first it was busy, but as she got further away from civilisation the traffic petered out in a satisfying way. At the brow of a hill the familiar rattle of a cattle grid made her smile. It was such an alien sound in this wild expanse of countryside. She was on open moorland now, with far-distant views of unknown tors, the sort of country she loved.

There were ponies in the distance as the land got wilder, and the black soil was wet from last night's rain. She wound down her window and let the peaty smell rush in, along with the evocative sound of a curlew's call in the distance.

She jumped as her mobile rang. An approaching lay-by was what she needed, and she pulled into it and stopped.

'Sandy?' She was delighted to hear her friend's voice. 'How are you? I was just thinking of you.'

'Oh, Caro.' Sandy sounded choked.

'Something wrong?'

'It's Bob's mum. She had a fall, a bad one.'

'Oh Sandy, that's terrible. Is she badly hurt?'

'She's in hospital. They say she's broken her hip. We don't know what to do.' Sandy was crying now; there was the sound of muffled voices, and then the stronger tones of Bob took over.

'It's bad, Caro.'

'I'm so sorry — '

'She's old, you see, and helpless. More so now that this has happened. We might have to think about getting her looked after professionally some-where else. We don't know yet, but it seems likely.'

'She's had an operation?'

'She's in theatre now.'

'Is there anything I can do to help? Shall I come — ?'

'There's nothing, but thanks. We have to wait, that's all. I'm taking Sandy home now for something to eat and to collect some things. It's a bad job,

Caro, but we thought you needed to know.'

He sounded tense, unlike his usual self, and no wonder. She found her hands shaking in sympathy. She had known the couple a long time; and Bob's mum, too. A lovely lady. She felt helpless, sitting here in a car in this quiet place, with the sunshine streaming over the soggy ground and a faint mist hovering over the horizon.

'Thanks, Bob,' she said, tears in her throat too. 'Give Sandy my love. Tell her I'll be in touch. And Bob, take care.'

'You too.'

For a moment she stared ahead, unseeing. Bob was close to his mother, and this was hitting him hard. Sandy, too.

They had been so excited about purchasing her house, the pair of them, and Sandy's imagination had run riot as she thought up ways to make the two properties into one so that Bob's mum could live in one part and yet not feel lonely. It sounded ideal for someone in normal health. But not now. Oh no, not now.

Poor Caro. And poor Rose, too.

But what was she thinking? That was a shameful thought at a time like this. Her house would sell eventually to someone else, even if it took months; but Bob's mum was frail and in pain, and Bob and Sandy desperately worried.

She set off again, humbled by her selfish thoughts. With no heart for house-hunting now, she took the first available road to Hovercombe.

Above her, she caught sight of a bird skimming the airways, and thought of Liam and the day they had spent together when he had taken her to The Green Beech Gallery for the first time and they had seen the picture of the sparrowhawk on the sign in the foyer. She had been captivated by his impromptu history lesson of how King John had settled on a sparrowhawk as a year's rent for the town of Moretonhampstead. She smiled now at the image of Liam's eager expression, and the way his eyes had shone at her obvious interest.

As she watched, the bird swooped, having spotted its prey. She was swept with sympathy until another thought took over. It was doing what birds of prey did naturally. Suddenly, she thought of Elissa back at Hovercombe Manor. Liam must have given her the authority to use his computer. Because of it, she had had the confidence to deal with Jared Butler in a way he understood.

Caro sighed. She had always felt confident in her ability to look out for Rose, to protect her when she needed it. But now she would be no use to her, apart from looking after Jonah to enable her to do a job she hated. She had wanted to provide financial security to save her from this. Now, in the short term, that wasn't possible. It was only too clear that she had failed.

* * *

As soon as she stepped out of the car, Caro knew that no one was at home at Hover Cottage. She must have picked up something in the air. There was no other clue. The same birds sang in the budding trees, and the same faint tractor noise faded into silence in the distance. At least, she supposed it was the same one from Bradfield's farm that they often heard working away when they were outside in the garden. She listened for a moment, and then opened the back of the car to remove her precious portfolio.

They hadn't seen much of young Evie lately, she thought. Something made her look up at that moment to see her coming up the lane from the farm in the same baggy jeans and light blue top she'd worn at the tenants' party. How strange was that? She was beginning to believe that this hidden valley was a magic place. How else would she have this premonition of things being not quite right when everything appeared just as normal as

226

at any other time? If Rose had taken Jonah to see his grandmother, there would be a note inside to say that was where they were, just as on any other normal day. And yet, for no reason, she felt a twinge of anxiety. It was irrational, but she felt it.

'I was coming to see Rose,' Evie said breathlessly as she reached her.

For a moment, Evie looked the vulnerable young child she must once have been. Then she brushed her long hair away from her face and straightened her shoulders.

'I need money.'

'Don't we all?'

'No, really, I mean it.' Evie looked ready to burst into tears. 'I'll earn it. I'll do anything.'

Caro made a move towards the gate.

'I've a feeling Rose is out. But we'll go and see, shall we?'

A purring welcome from Fluffy would have been nice, she thought, and the feel of his soft body rubbing against her legs to convince her that this wasn't some sort of dream. Like pinching herself to tell she was awake.

She rang the bell to make sure the place was empty, and then used her key. 'Come in, Evie, but I don't think she's here.'

Fluffy was, though, and looked up at them, blinking drowsily from his comfortable seat on the living room sofa.

At once, Evie was down on her knees, making such a fuss of him that Caro wondered he didn't object.

'Aren't you supposed to be at school?' she asked.

'Not today. It's an inset day.' Evie's voice was muffled in Fluffy's fur.

'I see. I'll make some tea in a minute. Would you like some? I'll just take my portfolio through to where I work.'

Evie looked up in surprise.

'You work? But they said . . . So you're not on holiday, then?' Her face brightened. 'Then who looks after Jonah?'

Light suddenly dawned, and Caro smiled. 'Ah, I see!'

'I'm free at weekends and it'll be half-term soon. There are exams after that, and then I won't have much to do.'

'You're making plans well ahead, then?'

Evie got up and brushed down her knees, although there was no need to as far as Caro could see. 'Someone has to.'

There was the sound of a door opening, and of Jonah's high-pitched voice. Rose didn't call out as she usually did. Caro went out into the hall and found her manoeuvring the push-chair into the porch before releasing Jonah.

'Is everything all right, Rose?'

Rose looked at her, eyes wide with apprehension. 'I got a text from Cindy. On the way home. I was going to call in and see her. She said not to bring Jonah, but I don't know why. There was something about Arnold. She sounded upset. I thought I could leave him with you so I could go and see if she's all right.'

'I'll drive you,' Caro said. 'Evie's here. She'll look after him.' She thought of Liam, still away from home. He had asked her to check on Elissa. This might involve her too, whatever it was, if Rose thought it was serious enough to investigate. 'Let's go.'

They could hear Evie's voice, and Jonah's answering squeals. Rose nodded. 'I'll just check how long Evie can stay.'

20

The back door that usually stood open was shut. By the side of the steps stood a milk crate, empty but for a pair of secateurs balanced across one corner.

Rose stared in dismay. 'That's not right.'

'Kevin's?'

'His best ones. He always keeps them in a drawer in the potting shed, and never lets them out of his sight.'

'Then he's somewhere about.'

Caro tried the door. It opened into an empty kitchen.

'The garden,' Rose said. 'That's where they'll be.'

In this sheltered place, the air was warm, and the growing things in the raised beds looked lush and green. Insects hummed, and there was the scent of freshly-picked mint.

Raised voices inside the building shattered the air. Caro had the sense that she had been here before. There were Cindy's threatening tones, and another voice as well as Kevin's.

'Arnold,' she said.

The next minute, the garden seemed to explode with noise as the three of them rushed out. Cindy waved her arms at Arnold, shouting abuse, while Kevin backed up against the wall. His eyes had a hunted look.

Caro stepped forward. 'Would someone explain what's going on?'

A moment's silence, and then all three started talking at once. From it, Caro gathered that Arnold was demanding something of Kevin that he didn't want to give.

'Tell him, Rose,' Cindy screeched, 'tell him you're not moving from your cottage.'

Arnold's face reddened as he glared at Rose. 'You don't mean it?'

'I do.'

'I made plans with the agent's

blessing. Kevin's input as cover is vital.' He tapped the side of his nose. 'Acquiring garden requirements, you might say. Other things good for a massive profit when we sell them on to Jared's connections.'

'But I don't see — '

'Well you wouldn't, an innocent like you.'

Rose flushed.

'But my cottage — '

'Needed for storage. Isolated but near enough. I need to be on the spot.'

'Not my spot.'

Kevin said nothing, but his face had paled.

'Or anyone else's spot, either,' Cindy's accusing voice rang out. 'You've been forcing him into it and I'm not having it. He's my man, is Kevin. Leave him alone.'

'And Cindy's my woman.' Kevin's voice was strong as he came to stand beside her.

Arnold's glance at the pair of them was withering.

'So you're not man enough, Kevin Masters, to stand up for yourself?'

Kevin thrust his shoulders back. 'And you're not man enough to accept a refusal when you hear one. It's not going to happen. And while we're at it, I want my secateurs back, wherever they are.'

Caro opened her mouth to tell him, but Arnold had vanished. Kevin was the first to move. 'I want those secateurs. Now.'

They found Arnold standing at the kitchen door, a stocky figure whose face was contorted in fury. He stepped forward. In his hand, he held the secateurs pointed towards them. Then, blind with rage, he hurled them.

There was a cry of warning from Cindy as she threw herself at Kevin. Then Rose slipped noiselessly to the ground with blood oozing through her torn jeans.

$\star$ $\star$ $\star$

Liam Tate set off from his business meeting in Bristol with a heart lighter than it had been for days. He'd had a tough time of it this last week, and needed this period on his own to mull over some of the details that had been put to him at the last moment. Driving down the M5 gave him this opportunity. So much to come to terms with. His accountant had stressed the importance of a speedy decision, and so he had stayed on in Bristol for extra time, and signed the contract when the clock in the hotel vestibule was striking eleven at night.

Mulvery Court was now his — or would be, as soon as the sale was completed. This startling development still had the power to make his mind whirl.

'Do you want it or don't you?' the irascible owner had demanded at last, taking him completely by surprise. A quick glance at the man's solicitor had confirmed the seriousness of the request, and without further thought the deed was done.

'I want it,' he had said, and immediately experienced a lightness of spirit that told him it was the right, though astonishing, decision.

So much for his original plan to persuade the owner to let the rights to the grounds on a long lease to give him the opportunity to expand some of his more revolutionary ideas, and to use it as a show-place to attract more work of the same kind. It was a tough assignment, but one to relish. Instead, he was the owner of the whole estate, with the freedom to do exactly as he chose to the grounds, without any imposed restraint.

The thought was awe-inspiring.

When he had first met the man briefly on the way home from Moreton-hampstead, he had picked up on the uncertainty in his eyes and the way his hands had trembled as he shut the door on them. Here was a worried man almost at breaking point. Afterwards, he had felt relaxed about the abortive visit, even though he had been far keener on his proposed plans than was normal in the circumstances. You won some, you lost some, and then you moved on. But not far in this case, as it turned out. A mere hour or so and then he was away again, driving off to Bristol which Gerald Montgomery, the owner, had decided was the place for the transaction he had in mind to take place. Eccentric to the last, the old gentleman hadn't turned up himself until yesterday. Days of negotiations with the owner's men of business had ended at last, and now the Mulvery estate was his and already his head was swirling with ideas.

He had toyed with the idea of driving home last night, but soon rejected it. He was feeling shattered and needed to get his head down, so setting out in the morning was a better option. He glanced now at the clock. He was making good progress. It occurred to him that he'd eaten nothing since an early dinner the evening before, and that he was in danger of becoming light-headed if he didn't do something about it.

Taunton Deane Services seemed an attractive prospect, and as he pulled in he saw that the car park was almost empty. He would linger in the restaurant here for a while in comfort, and get some of those ideas of his down on paper while they were fresh in his mind.

He got out of the car and thought instantly of Caro. A different service station, a different place, but the vision of her pale face and vulnerability at the particular moment of their first meeting stirred him with a sharpness that took him by surprise. Soon he would be back at Hovercombe where only the sound of birds and the wind in the trees and the distant bark of a dog stirred the quiet air. There would be a feeling of homecoming that would wrap him round in a way he knew was for him. That visit to Moretonhampstead nearly ten days ago had been life-changing for both of them. An enchanted morning driving up onto the moor with the haze rising from the distant hills and larks singing above. Caro had been delighted with The Green Beech Gallery, and Olivia had seen her potential at once. Definitely a future here for her there if she chose to take it.

When at last he was ready to leave, he felt for the button on the dashboard to set the roof in motion and then hesitated. The good meal he had eaten at leisure had done nothing to clear his head, and that was strange. He wanted to be home, but now something was making him pause to consider. Hovercombe Manor felt close and yet distant, and he couldn't understand it. On this occasion, the roof would stay closed. For some reason it felt safer.

21

At once Caro was down at Rose's side, ripping the hole in her jeans bigger, and then pulling out a handkerchief from her pocket to stem the flow of blood. 'Towels, Cindy, and be quick.'

Arnold, his face ashen, sank down beside them. 'I didn't mean — '

'It's all right,' sobbed Rose, struggling to sit up. 'I got in the way.'

'Stay still.' Caro was murmuring words of comfort as Rose's pallor intensified. Then she snatched at the towels Cindy brought. 'I think it's stopping now. I hope so. I was afraid — '

'I'll ring for the ambulance,' Kevin said.

'No, no, wait. Let's see how bad it is first.'

Caro removed the towels, and they could see that, although the wound appeared deep, it wasn't the huge slash they had expected. The tip of the secateurs had caught the fleshy part of Rose's thigh, and although blood was oozing out it wasn't looking so threatening now.

Cindy leaned forward for a closer look. 'It might need stitches.'

'A&E, then,' Kevin said. 'I'll drive.'

Arnold sprang to his feet. 'No, I will.'

Kevin shot him a scornful glance. 'No way. That's my job.'

'Let's get her inside and get it washed,' Caro said. 'You've a first-aid kit handy, Cindy? A dressing's needed.'

Caro got to her feet and helped Rose up too. For a moment, Rose swayed a little, and clung on to her.

'I'll be all right,' she murmured. 'It . . . it was an accident.'

'Accident?' said Kevin, his face white. 'That was no accident. Those secateurs were dirty. She could be infected.'

'Don't worry, Arnold,' Rose murmured. 'I'll be all right. I just need to get home. Jonah — '

Arnold looked unconvinced, and hung back as Caro and Kevin between them helped Rose through the gate and into the kitchen. By the time the dressing was in place, he had gone.

'Coward,' Cindy said, standing back and surveying the scene. 'Where did he go, Kevin?'

'To warn his mate Butler.'

'Good riddance.'

'Tea all round, I think.'

'No A& E,then?'

'Tea first.' Cindy was already dealing with it.

A sense of unreality was creeping over Caro. She hardly realised when Cindy handed her a mug, and drank her tea so hot that her throat burned.

'I'll pick you up at the front door. That's the easiest. I'll get the van.'

They both got up.

In the hall, Elissa met them. Her eyebrows shot up in surprise. 'I thought I heard Liam.'

Caro had forgotten Elissa in the recent events. 'Liam?'

'Expected back at any moment.'

'News to me,' Cindy said bitterly.

'I'm telling you now,' Elissa said, her voice crisp. 'Is something going on here I should know about?'

There were definite sounds of a vehicle outside now. Elissa's eyes brightened. 'Liam? Here he is now!'

Caro paused, and for a moment stood quite still.

Then he was with them, suitcase in hand, looking somehow taller in his dark suit. He stopped, surprised, and loosened his tie.

'What's going on?'

Elissa rushed to him. 'That's just what I wanted to know, and they won't tell me.'

'I suspect this isn't the moment. We'll talk later, Elissa. There's a lot for us to discuss.'

She looked at the others. 'I'm his right-hand woman,' she said proudly.

Liam appeared not to hear. Instead, he was staring at Caro. 'But surely that's blood?'

She looked down at her jacket, and saw the darker spots she hadn't yet noticed. 'Oh, yes. You see, it was Rose.'

His expression as he saw the dressing on Rose's leg was inscrutable. 'An accident? How did that happen? Am I missing something here?'

Cindy said, ignoring him, 'Get off to A&E, the two of you. Kevin's been waiting long enough. There's been enough damage done here already.'

'I'm the one to see to this,' Liam said. 'Kevin's in no fit state to drive anywhere. Save the recriminations for later.'

'There'll be plenty of those,' Cindy said darkly, glaring at Elissa. 'I'll give her 'right-hand woman'!'

'See to Kevin, Cindy. He needs you. And don't argue.' Liam sounded stern, but the expression in his eyes as they rested on Caro indicated otherwise. 'Come on. Let me help you, Rose. My car's right by the door. Can you manage to get that far?'

Caro settled Rose on the back seat of Liam's Volvo, where she could stretch her leg out and lean back in comfort. Then she backed out of the vehicle, clutching the pair of baggy jeans from the laundry basket that Cindy had thrust at her with a muttered, 'Take these for her. She'll need them.' Liam was holding the passenger door open, and she slipped inside with a murmured word of thanks. As they set off, she pulled out her mobile.

'I'd better check on Jonah. Evie Barnet is looking after him at the cottage.'

At once Evie's clear voice rang out so that even Rose was able to hear what she said and be reassured.

'Tell her there's food in the fridge and to help herself,' Rose whispered.

Caro had already thought of that.

She clicked off and leaned back in her seat, unaware of anything more except for one thought that wouldn't go away. Elissa was Liam's *right-hand woman*. The words rang mockingly in her ears.

The coffee machine was doing overtime. It was something to have to queue to get drinks out of a machine in a cardboard cup, Caro thought as she edged her way along. This was their third coffee of the morning — the fourth in her case, if you counted the one that Cindy had insisted she drink before setting out for the hospital, except that that one had been tea. No, the fifth. The Green Beech Gallery in Olivia's tasteful china. How long ago that seemed. It must be past lunchtime now, and Rose had been gone for ages.

The staff here had been so kind. Knowing that professionals were taking over was a huge relief, however long they had to wait, and the seats in the reception area were comfortable. Liam had organised coffee for them at once, and had talked soothingly to Rose. By the time she was called in, the colour had returned to her cheeks.

Only then did he question Caro closely, wanting to know every last detail that could throw some light on how it was that a member of his staff should sustain such an injury from someone who was related to her. She couldn't fully understand it herself, except that Arnold had thrown the secateurs in a fit of rage and Rose had been in the way. She had closed her eyes, remembering, and at once was back there in the yard with the breeze in her hair and shocked faces around her and Rose lying on the ground and blood —

'Enough of this for the time being.' His voice sounded anxious.

'I'm fine,' she said as she opened her eyes, ashamed of her momentary weakness.

'More coffee, I think, and then I'll tell you what I've been getting up to while I've been away.'

It was certainly something she hadn't expected, and she looked at him in wonder as he told her of his recent surprising acquisition of the Mulvery Court estate. It was such astonishing news that it was hard to take in. She listened carefully as Liam expounded on his ideas for the grounds that were amazing too, as she told him, one whose love of spacious lawns and colourful borders hadn't changed since she was a little girl visiting National Trust gardens on visits to her Sussex grandparents.

'No trees?' he teased.

'Oh yes, trees. I'd forgotten them.'

He smiled. 'Plenty of them at Mulvery Court. My ultra-modern designs will incorporate them.'

'And the house?'

'Ah yes, the house. Now there's a question.'

She thought of the ugly building and the overgrown garden, and wondered at Liam's enthusiasm.

He leaned forward. 'All I know is that some time ago the place was converted into holiday flats. Not very well, I gather, but that remains to be seen.

Cindy might be the right person to consult about that. Another coffee?'

'I'll get it this time.'

Now, as she stood in the queue, she thought that by the time she returned his active mind would have come up with plans that anyone else would have taken a long time to consider. She wasn't sure how Cindy fitted in. And what about Kevin? Maybe Elissa would like the idea and be as enthusiastic about it as he wished, but somehow she couldn't imagine it. Contrasted with Hovercombe Manor, it fell far short.

She carried the cardboard cups of steaming liquid back to where Liam was sitting in the seats near a low table. He stood up and took one from her.

'Thanks, Caro.'

'Surely Rose'll be out soon?'

He smiled. 'You're getting impatient.'

'Impatient? It's two o'clock.'

'Like me to tell you more about my plans for Mulvery Court?'

'There's more?'

'There's always more. I'm preparing to bore you.'

'You'd never do that.' She stopped, confused. What was she thinking of? Far too personal. She sat down, careful not to spill her drink as she moved her chair away from his a little. She was beginning to feel woozy and closed her eyes again, again seeing Rose in her mind, and registering her anxiety that Arnold shouldn't blame himself for her injury when he was entirely at fault.

'I'll take a wander round and look for some food.' Liam's voice seemed to come from a distance. 'Are you all right, Caro, for a few minutes? I won't be long.'

She didn't question where he got the sandwiches, but ate hers thankfully, and immediately felt better. She looked at this kind man who had done all he could to help in a difficult situation. She was glad she hadn't told him of the likely falling-through of the sale of her house. She wasn't going to tout for sympathy. Until now, she had forgotten

Olivia's offer of an exhibition, but that piece of news could wait as well.

Rose was ready to go soon after that, almost unrecognisable in Cindy's baggy jeans. She had instructions to rest at home between the visits of the community nurse who apparently would be keeping an eye on her.

At Hover Cottage, Jonah greeted his mother with squeals of joy, and had to be restrained as he tried to climb on her lap. Laughing, Rose blew him a kiss. 'Have you been a good boy for Evie?'

Evie answered for him. 'He's been great. And I can come any time you need me.'

'Evie, book. Look, Mummy.'

'I'm looking.'

Liam drew Caro to one side, saying he'd give Evie a lift home.

'And I shall be taking care of payment to her now and in the future,' he said, in a tone that left no room for argument. 'I'm at fault for giving Jared Butler the benefit of the doubt in the way I did. I should have hardened my heart at the first sign that he was taking too much on himself.'

Caro thought instantly of the poor bullied Jared growing up with his alcoholic mother. 'You allowed your knowledge of his background to cloud your judgement, that's all.'

Liam shrugged. 'A poor decision on my part.'

'Or human sympathy.'

He smiled suddenly and patted her arm. 'I wish I could agree with you.'

'It was Arnold Beesley too,' she said. 'Tom's cousin. They had hatched a plot between them, and it was he who hurt Rose.'

'I have a feeling that you won't be seeing any more of him. Or of Jared Butler either when I've finished with him. And for the moment, I feel the need to look out for my new cafe overseer. D'you think Rose would like to change jobs, or rather combine that with serving sometimes in the garden shop? She'll be an asset, a charming girl like Rose.'

'But Elissa?'

His smile deepened. 'I have other plans for her.'

Caro's heart thudded and she couldn't look at him. It sounded like a warning and struck at her heart. She swallowed hard.

'Yes, I see. And thank you for all your help, Liam. You've been great.'

And then he and Evie were gone, and she felt empty and alone.

22

Kevin called to see them the next day, bringing a basket of goodies from Cindy. These included Jonah's favourite dumbo cakes, and something that brought tears to Caro's eyes: a clockwork mouse for Fluffy. She held it in her hand, a ridiculous thing to inspire such a reaction. She must be feeling weak or overwrought or something. She wiped her eyes, turned the key, and then put the mouse down close to her cat where it zoomed off across the room.

Jonah shrieked with laughter. 'More, more, more,' he cried as Fluffy shot after it. 'Me now.'

This kept them both amused for some time, so that Kevin could fill Caro and Rose in on what had been happening at the Manor.

'Elissa's gone,' he said. 'Early this morning, but we were there to see her off and thank her for the gifts she gave us. She's left one for you as well, Caro.' He felt in his pocket and produced a package wrapped in gold paper.

Rose craned forward to look as Caro opened it up to reveal a small box. On the lid in tiny handwriting were the words: *This belonged to my grandmother and I want you to have it. It's not valuable. Please don't thank me.*

'What is it?' breathed Rose.

Caro opened the box. Inside, on a bed of cotton wool, lay a small pink pendant in the shape of a bird on a delicate silver chain. She lifted it out.

'It's beautiful!'

'Put it on, Caro. Here let me do it up for you.'

Caro sat down beside her on the sofa and waited while Rose, breathing heavily in concentration, fixed the clasp. Then she got up and moved to the mirror on the wall opposite the window. She rarely wore jewellery of any kind, but this looked good against the cream of her shirt. She looked critically at her hair, and ran her hands through it to fluff it up. As she moved, the reflected sunlight in the glass highlighted the uneven surface of the pendant so that it looked for a moment like some glowing precious jewel.

She gazed in wonder that the small plain mirror she had hardly registered before should do this. There was magic in everything if you stopped to look, and there certainly was in this unexpected gift from someone she had thought disliked her.

Reluctantly she left the mirror and sat down again.

'She's given Liam a huge present, one you can't see.' Kevin was saying. He grinned.

Rose looked interested. 'And what's that?'

'He's going to tell us about it later. She'll be back, of course, before long. Liam has big plans, and needs to get them agreed now. Cindy's all for it.' He beamed with pride. 'I told her to go for it. She won't get a chance like this again.'

'So, what's that?' Rose asked. She was leaning back on the sofa now with her leg up on a low stool and looked totally relaxed.

'You've heard of this place Mulvery Court that Liam's got? Needs a lot doing to it, he says, and he wants Cindy to be in charge. What d'you think of that? There's a flat there she can use, big enough for two if it came to that.' He broke off, a flush spreading over his good-natured face.

'But what about the Manor? Isn't she needed there?'

'Apparently she won't be. Not now.'

Caro had heard enough. She slipped out of the room, got her jacket from its peg in the hall, and went outside. The breeze was cool on her face. She'd spoken on the phone to Sandy this morning to ask how things were and to show her support, but now she had a strong urge to go back to Bridport and see it for herself. If only she could just get into her car and drive! For the next few days, Rose needed her more than ever, but Evie was free again at the weekend and would look after Jonah then. It was becoming increasingly obvious that the cottage was too small to contain someone like herself who needed room to spread out with all the exhibition work on hand. She needed peace of mind too, and to distance herself from Hovercombe Manor. Rose, as well, must feel inhibited with her spare room taken up as well as a large part of her dining area.

She looked at the surrounding trees and fields and the hills that had always seemed so protective but now felt as if they were closing in on her. She could no longer do her best work here for the longing to be with Liam. The pain would be there always, but distance might help her get it into perspective. Until she found a purchaser for her house, she could return there, and hope that when her part-exhibition opened at The Green Beech Gallery, she could come back for the duration of that to do her share of stewarding. By that time, a property on the other side of the moor might prove suitable if a studio workplace at the gallery was available to rent so that she didn't need a studio in the house. That should make house-hunting easier. She would be closer to Rose and Jonah than in her present place, and available for looking after Jonah sometimes. She had overcome setbacks before, and would do so again.

She sighed, and with a heavy heart went back indoors.

*   *   *

Packing up her belongings was a dismal job during the next few days. Caro stopped every now and again to gaze out of the window at the view she'd come to know so well. Rose had taken Jonah to visit his grandmother again today, so the usual sounds about the cottage were missing. In the deep silence, Caro imagined she heard a faint sighing, as if the trees outside were in sympathy with her as she prepared to leave Hover Cottage for the foreseeable future.

But that was being melodramatic, and she gave herself a mental shake. Not much more to do now; only her painting gear, and that wouldn't take long. Rose had persuaded her to leave Fluffy behind and she had agreed, knowing how much Jonah loved having him around. She suspected that Rose was hoping that Fluffy would be the means of drawing Caro back more quickly, and wanted him as a sort of hostage. She smiled as she thought of it. She had promised to come back very soon, but was loath to commit herself more than that. Evie Barnet was looking forward to be with Jonah at weekends when needed, and during the Easter holidays. Until then, Evie's mother was happy to stand in for her daughter.

So, tomorrow she would be off.

* * *

'So, what are you doing here?'

Caro had stopped for fuel at Exeter Services. She drove into the car park and saw Liam's car following her with a jolt of recognition. He parked in the empty space beside hers and leapt out, unsmiling, his eyebrows raised. Usually this signalled some light-hearted remark, but not this time. He was looking at her with his head thrown back and with a serious expression on his face. Her heart lurched.

'I'm on the way somewhere,' he said, 'like you, Caro. Something of importance I felt I needed to do.'

She thought she understood what he was trying to say, but acknowledging it was more than she could manage. A strange lethargy was creeping over her.

'I'm on my way to see my house.'

'To check that it's still there?' The muscle at one side of his mouth moved slightly.

'The sale is falling through, and it's a blow. How can I be of use to Rose with no money to spare? She needs me to . . . ' She broke off, listening to her own words and wondering for the first time exactly what she meant by them. That forlorn look that Rose had worn since Tom died had gone. Rose had found her niche. She was an employee at the Manor in her own right, and felt closer to Tom because of it.

Caro knew now, with a suddenness that was overpowering, that she couldn't go back to her old life away from Rose and Jonah. She needed them as much as they needed her. They were family, and she wanted to be close to them for her own sake. She took a deep breath, and for a moment the ground seemed to sway. Liam put out a hand to steady her.

'I think we'll have that coffee you turned down on our first meeting all those weeks ago.'

'You followed me here?'

'Rose told me where you were going, Caro, and why. She was concerned. And rightly so, it seems. She was looking out for you.'

This was an incredible thought, too: Rose looking out for her, instead of the other way around!

'But Elissa — ?'

'Ah yes, Elissa. A good friend repaying an old debt, as she saw it.'

The entrance to the amenities was some distance away, and as they walked towards it, Liam said, 'Elissa knew I wished to expand, hopefully in Devon where I was now to be living. She intervened with her grandfather, the owner of Mulvery Court.'

'That old man is her grandfather?'

He grinned. 'Not much of a family likeness there, is there?'

'Hearts of gold, I suppose, the pair of them. He must be fond of her.'

'That, I wouldn't know, but it seems likely. He's going to move somewhere more suitable for this stage in his life, where he'll be looked after properly. And Elissa . . . well, she has her own career to follow.'

'I'm not too sure what that is.'

'Who knows, with Elissa? Something

unexpected, I should think. That's the way she is.'

Unexpected, yes, Caro thought with a glow of warmth, remembering the pretty pendant she had been wearing ever since Elissa had sent it to her.

'But she'll come for visits,' Liam said. 'If you agree, that is.'

She was confused. 'Me?'

He smiled wryly. 'I'm jumping ahead of myself. Come on, where's that coffee?'

They were in the light and warmth and cheerful noise of the service station now. Around them, the crowds bustled. Liam took her arm again and steered her towards the far side. There were empty tables behind a protruding wall, and from here the sounds were muted to a soft drone. He chose a table by the long expanse of glass. Outside were lawns and trees, and they could have been miles from anywhere.

'This will do.'

She sank down on the chair he pulled out for her. The coffee came in huge cups, and was hot and strong. She slipped her arms out of her jacket and straightened the pendant.

He looked surprised. 'But surely — '

'Elissa gave it to me,' she said.

'I've seen her wear it. She told me that the sparrowhawk represents the emblem for Mulvery Court. It's used on the letterheads of the business transactions the solicitor produced for me to sign.'

'The sparrowhawk again. An important bird.'

'In this case, yes, and Elissa knew it. She's quite a girl.' He was silent for a moment, looking down at his coffee, deep in thought.

Caro fingered the pendant, liking the rough texture of the bird, aware now that Elissa had sent her a significant message.

Liam looked up. 'Her present to me was a promise to update and oversee my website to include my plans for Mulvery Court, and the residential courses in land management and design

I have in mind. Other courses too, in due time, with your interests in mind. Financially, it will be a strain for the first year or two, but it can be done.'

She was certain of that too. He had the enthusiasm and drive needed for such a project. And talent as well. She would help him all she could.

'My friend next door is having to pull out of my house purchase,' she said, 'because Bob's mother has broken her hip.'

'Bob?'

'Her husband. They were going to convert my house into a place for her, but now they don't know what's going to happen. They can't commit themselves at the moment.'

She paused, gazing beyond him to the swaying trees. Who knew what the future held for any of them? Not Sandy and Bob, previously excited about the chance to have his mother near, and now most likely having to relinquish that plan. Not Aunt Maggie, who didn't know the guilt Caro would feel about her generous inheritance.

Liam picked up his cup and then put it down again. 'That's understandable, in the circumstances.'

'Well, yes.'

'So it's still on the market?

She nodded, and thought of the houses she had viewed that were all unsuitable for her. Having cash available would be an advantage so she could go ahead immediately if she needed to, but somehow that didn't seem so important now. She was surprised by her sudden sense of freedom.

'Then why not take it off the market and wait for a while? You don't know for sure about your friend's circumstances, and they may change. It seems she's been very fair to you.'

'Sandy's always been a good friend.'

He nodded. 'And things sort themselves out in the end. You don't really need to do anything.'

'But where will I live meanwhile?'

'There's plenty of room at the Manor.'

She sat perfectly still.

'Caro?'

The silence was like a wall between them. He picked up a spoon, stirred coffee that didn't need to be stirred, and all the time she watched the ripples on the surface until they faded away.

'We've known each other, what . . . a few weeks?' he murmured. 'A few significant weeks in my life — and, I hope, in yours.'

She gazed at him, wanting to believe the implications in his words but not quite daring to.

'And this wasn't the place I would have chosen.'

'It's a beautiful place.'

His face lit up with a smile. 'You think so?'

'Of course.' She gave him a radiant smile too. His hand clasped hers on the table, and she looked at it, wondering how it had got there unnoticed. She felt the pressure of his fingers and it felt good.

'My beautiful Caro.' He leaned forward and his lips softly touched hers.

The next moment she was in his arms with her face buried in his chest. She felt his heart beating beneath his shirt and the moment was magic.

She knew her face was flushed and her hair awry as he released her. They were no longer alone, but she didn't care. Tables were being occupied. There was the clatter of dishes and the hot smell of chips and beefburgers. A child cried and was hushed.

'We need somewhere even more beautiful than this,' he said, his mouth turning up at the corners. 'Becky Falls. D'you know it? A suitable beauty spot to ask you to marry me. What d'you say?'

She smiled as she took his hand. There was no need for words, and he didn't wait for any as he bent and kissed her again.

We do hope that you have enjoyed reading this large print book.

Did you know that all of our titles are available for purchase?

We publish a wide range of high quality large print books including:
Romances, Mysteries, Classics
General Fiction
Non Fiction and Westerns

Special interest titles available in large print are:
The Little Oxford Dictionary
Music Book, Song Book
Hymn Book, Service Book

Also available from us courtesy of Oxford University Press:
Young Readers' Dictionary
(large print edition)
Young Readers' Thesaurus
(large print edition)

For further information or a free brochure, please contact us at:
Ulverscroft Large Print Books Ltd.,
The Green, Bradgate Road, Anstey,
Leicester, LE7 7FU, England.
Tel: (00 44) **0116 236 4325**
Fax: (00 44) **0116 234 0205**

A HEART'S WAGER

Heidi Sullivan

Eva Copperfield has lived a life of poverty in the squalid slums of New York — until a sudden inheritance gives her the chance of a new life as lady of the manor in the English countryside. Her journey from rags to riches is complicated by the mysterious Ben — who is either a lord or a charlatan! Eva has to navigate the Atlantic and her heart before she can find a home . . . and love. Wagers are being made. Who will win?

MALLORCAN MAGIC

Jill Barry

On the rebound from a broken engagement, romance is the last thing on Eira's mind as she treats herself to a holiday in Mallorca. But two chance encounters with handsome entrepreneur Danny Carpenter, followed by a job offer as his children's nanny, set her on an entirely unexpected path. Soon she must deal not only with the complicated issue of falling for her employer, but also of coming to his defence when he is arrested and taken into custody for a crime he is certainly innocent of committing . . .

CAN'T BUY ME LOVE

Jo Weeks

When Jane Duncan's beloved grandmother died, she left Jane the cottage in the little Scottish village where she had spent so many happy hours as a child. Relieved to leave the city life behind, Jane soon moved in. Her grandparents had lovingly tended the neighbouring Shaws estate as housekeeper and head gardener for many years. But Shaws has just been sold to Connor Macaulay, a wealthy American businessman whose plans could mean the end of everything Jane holds dear. Sparks fly when they meet . . .

THE SILVER LINING

Wendy Kremer

Lady Stratton and her daughter Julia are living in straitened circumstances near the de Vere estate. When Gareth de Vere crashes his phaeton outside their cottage, he mistakes Julia for the maid. Although their attraction to each other grows with further encounters, their different social standings make it a mismatch. And despite a plot to provoke Gareth's feelings by his dissolute cousin, Fenton, Julia knows there is no chance of overcoming their circumstances — she is destined to love in vain . . .